((REBOUND))

BOB KRECH

MARSHALL CAVENDISH

For my family

Text copyright © 2006 by Bob Krech

Marshall Cavendish Corporation
99 White Plains Road
Tarrytown, NY 10591
www.marshallcavendish.us

Library of Congress Cataloging-in-Publication Data

Krech, Bob.

Rebound / by Bob Krech.

p. cm.

Summary: Determined to make the varsity basketball team, seventeen-year-old Ray finds his efforts to play

both hindered and helped by the atmosphere of racism in his town.

ISBN-13: 978-0-7614-5319-2

ISBN-10: 0-7614-5319-9

[1. Basketball—Fiction. 2. Racism—Fiction. 3. Race relations—Fiction.] I. Title.

PZ7.K8768Re 2006

[Fic]—dc22

2006001462

The text of this book is set in ACaslon.
Book design by Alex Ferrari/ferraridesign.com

Printed in China
First edition
10 9 8 7 6 5 4 3

mc Marshall Cavendish

table of contents

"They told me that it was all black and white
There's so many shades I can see boys."
—Graham Parker, "Back to Schooldays"

prologue
SHEEP AND GOATS

The tiles on the locker-room floor felt like rows of little ice cubes under my bare feet. Even though it was the second week of November there was definitely no heat on. I always feel cold when I'm nervous anyway. And I was nervous. I had never tried out for a basketball team before.

The other nervous thing was I was surrounded by half-naked bodies: coal black, tan, chocolate brown. It looked like every black kid in the school was going out for the team. And then me. Pale skin, long nose, sandy brown hair, and a cowlick that won't stay down. I don't know what I expected, but it wasn't being the *only* white guy. I changed pretty quick and got myself out of there.

The guidance counselors and teachers are always telling you, we're all the same: black, white, Chinese, doesn't matter. All you have to do is look to see that's not exactly true. Our lips are different, hair is different, noses, skin, talking, even smell. I don't mind the differences. To tell you the truth, I think it's interesting and kind of cool, but there are definitely differences.

Out on the gym floor there was a swarm of guys shooting like twenty balls on two hoops. Everybody was yelling, pushing, and falling over one another under the baskets trying to get a rebound.

No one else from my neighborhood was going out for basketball. If you live in Greenville and are into sports, you wrestle. We're big, strong, tough, hardheaded Polacks in our part of town! And we tear people up on the mat to prove it. It's like a tradition. I only got into b-ball in eighth grade because my uncle Greg, who's a cop in the next town over, needed one more kid to play on his Police Athletic League team, the Bridgeton PAL Falcons. I had no idea what I was doing, but he asked me, so I went. And I got hooked. I loved the constant motion. The excitement in your stomach when you sink a shot. I couldn't stop playing. Even so, I really stunk at first. You didn't have to try out for the Falcons. They were happy to get anybody.

While I edged my way in under the basket looking for a rebound, these two white kids, Ziggy Cryna and Richie Delorenzo, walked out of the locker room together. Even though they're from somewhere in North Franklin and I hardly knew them, I felt my chest and shoulders relax.

I managed to grab a rebound and take a quick shot. It skidded off the back rim. A whistle pierced the racket. All the balls immediately stopped bouncing. Every head turned. Malovic appeared on the sidelines. He's a middle-aged guy. Looks kind of like a hawk, with a beaky nose, glasses, and pretty short hair. He was wearing baggy gray sweats and high black Nikes with a red swoosh. Now with him there, that made four of us who were white. "Line up on the end line," he called. "Quickly."

Everyone jogged over. I scooted in next to Ziggy on the line. He's got a round face, brushed up hair, and a big smile. I heard he's good. He whispered, "Hey, Ray."

"Hey, Zig. Richie."

Richie, tall and dark, just nodded. We all kept our eyes on Malovic.

At the time Malovic *was* the Franklin High basketball program. He coached the varsity and the junior varsity, which is pretty unusual. My cousin Sondra kept telling me what a nice guy he was. How he was her guidance counselor and he was real understanding and all. That didn't mean much to me except that maybe if he was such a nice guy and real understanding he'd put me on the team.

I'd been preparing for this tryout for a year. Two years, really. I wanted to play serious basketball on a real team. I was the best player on the Falcons, but we were not exactly topflight competition. I had to play a lot of PAL ball before I felt like I was ready to go out for Franklin High. That's why I waited till sophomore year. I wanted to be sure I was ready. I didn't want to be embarrassed. Or get cut.

I practiced every day before and after school in my driveway. Cold. Hot. Rain. Didn't matter. I did layups, thirty with the right hand and thirty with the left. If I missed one, I'd start all over. Then I'd shoot from the corners, work my way around the perimeter of the court. Miss? Start right back at the beginning. Bank shots, running one-hand hooks, everything. Same routine. Twice a day.

Malovic blew the whistle again and said, "Line backs. Till I say stop. Ready. Begin!"

My heart was pounding as I sprinted up the court. But the running was good. It helped me get out some of my nervousness, and I was one of the fastest. I hoped Malovic noticed this.

We did three sets of line backs. Then while we all stood there doubled over, sucking in the air, Malovic said, "Okay. We're going to do layups. Go right side, then switch to your left when I tell you. Half of you stay down here, other half on the other basket." His voice was kind of high and whiny.

We meandered into two groups, lined up, and started. I made all of my layups, left- and right-handed. A lot of guys were missing with their left. Badly. I started feeling that this might work out.

We did two different passing drills after that. No problem there. I was warmed up and loose. After that we shot jumpers off a pass from the foul line and I nailed four out of four. Better than anyone on my end of the court. Now I was thinking, yeah, I'm going to be playing ball for the Franklin Red Storm. I could see myself in that red and black uniform.

Then we started this ballhandling drill where you have to dribble from one end of the court to the other against an opponent. I got matched up with this small kid with a shaved head. His head was actually shining under the gym lights like somebody had buttered it. He had this habit of sticking his tongue out, too, while he was playing. You really noticed because his skin was so black it made his tongue look really pink, like baby-toy pink.

I got the ball first and started trying to bring it up around him, but he had some incredible fast hands. It was all I could do to just keep it away from him. Forget moving it forward. I couldn't get five feet up the floor before the whistle blew to change places.

On *his* first turn, he faked once, then went right around me and shot up the court like a laser beam. Never even looked back. Just dropped the ball there for me on the end line.

I tried again. He immediately smacked the ball out-of-bounds. I picked it up, hustled back onto the court, and started again. He slapped it right out again. While I chased it, he stood there with his hands on his hips looking at the ceiling. I was hoping nobody was seeing this.

I was sweating from embarrassment more than anything. The rest of the guys were working against each other in the middle of the floor, and I was chasing the ball out-of-bounds. I tried again. This time he flicked the ball away, grabbed it, and dribbled the full court the other way while I stood there. Malovic had told us specifically not to do that. "Don't steal the ball," he'd said. "Just stop your opponent's progress."

I looked over to see if Malovic was catching all this, and

he was staring straight at us. He just told us *not* to do this and the kid was doing it right in front of him, but Malovic didn't say a thing. I got the ball back and the kid did the same thing *again*. Stole it and dribbled away. And this time he shot a layup at the other end! I felt helpless and stupid standing there watching him.

Finally, mercifully, Malovic blew the whistle and had us all line up again. He walked directly over to us. "Robert—" he began.

The little baldhead guy looked up. I figured, all right, this is where this punk was going to get it for being a hot dog.

"—way to hustle." Malovic gave him a nod.

Unbelievable! Instead of bawling him out, he complimented him. What was going on with that?

Malovic called out, "Time for scrimmages. Count off by fives."

Okay. I tried to shake it off. Scrimmages are what really count anyway. That's where you can show how you do in a game situation.

The first time I was on the court, we ran for ten minutes, and I never touched the ball. No pass to me, no rebound, nothing. I just ran back and forth and guarded my guy on defense. I got to see this Robert in action on the other team, though, and he must have had three-quarters of their points. He was obviously the resident superstar, but a show-off and ball hog, dribbling behind his back and shooting every time he touched the ball.

While I was watching the other squads scrimmage, I noticed Malovic standing there chatting and nodding and laughing with this group of guys. It was like they were all old pals. Maybe he was their guidance counselor or something. My guidance counselor was Mr. Pinto. The bowling coach.

Second time my team got on, I got matched up with Robert because everybody else was smart enough and quick enough to match up with someone else. So, here was a good chance for me to stop Big Deal Robert in front of Malovic.

Robert immediately brought the ball up over the half line. I squared up on him. I was watching to see if he was going to go left or right, when he suddenly charged straight at me. He was going to plow right into me and put us both on the floor. I braced for the impact, ready to hang tough and take the charge, but at the last possible second he skipped the ball through my legs, picked it up behind me, and laid it up and in.

Guys on the sidelines screamed, "Ooooh!" Like they were in pain.

Malovic called over, "Very nice move."

This other kid on Robert's team was hooting and laughing like a hyena. He was tall and thin with some kind of gelled-up hair. I was pretty sure his name was Rudy. He was yelling and pointing at me, "Robert used you up! He used you *up!*"

Robert wagged his head back and forth laughing to himself. I wished I was playing football so I could tackle them both and knock the laughter right out of them.

Instead I just ran up the court on offense.

Malovic had us finish the tryout by shooting around. The manager, this real skinny kid named Powell, was walking around with a clipboard during the warm-down. He stopped next to Robert who was sitting on the end line near me. Apparently Robert was too cool to warm down. He just sat down.

I could hear Powell ask, "What's your shoe size?"

In this deep, croaky voice Robert said, "Seven."

Powell wrote something and walked over to this huge guy, Tyrone, and asked him the same thing. Then he went to Gel Head. Then Ziggy. I was thinking what is this shoe size thing about, but then it dawned on me—it was how you knew if you made the team. I slid over near Powell and tried to catch his eye, in case he might have missed me or didn't know my name, but he just kept going around talking to other guys. Finally, he handed the clipboard to Malovic.

I found out later that every guy on the team got a free pair of game shoes. High black leather Nikes with the red swoosh. Like Malovic was wearing.

Malovic blew the whistle and said, "Okay, let's bring it in. Take a seat in the middle." We all walked over and sat on the floor while he went down on one knee. "Okay, everybody. Good job today. Good hustle. I really wish I could use you all, but I can only keep twenty-two players. You know who you are. Have a seat over on the bleachers now."

The happy twenty-two went bopping over to the bleachers, slapping hands, talking, and smiling. Ziggy was up there with them. The rest of us were left sitting like a pile of garbage in the middle of the floor.

Richie was sitting next to me, shaking his head. Malovic focused on us garbage-types and said, "Now, I want you to remember. Everyone gets a fair shot to make this team. I encourage you to keep practicing, keep developing your games, and come out again next year." He stood up.

We all did too. "Good luck this year, gentlemen. Now, hit the showers."

We dragged ourselves into the locker room. It was pretty quiet except for some locker doors slamming. From out on the gym floor I could hear more yelling and laughing.

I felt rotten, but I couldn't complain too much. I hadn't exactly *earned* a spot on the team. I messed up on some stuff, but I didn't think the whole thing was particularly fair, either. That and Malovic didn't need to separate "the sheep from the goats" right in the middle of the gym in front of everybody. He could have put up a list or something.

But I was going to work on my game. I loved the game. It was the other junk like the sheep and goats and the playing favorites I didn't like. I was beginning to not like Malovic particularly, either.

Or this Robert kid.

chapter one
AT THE EGG STAND

"House." I point at the picture in the book and say it again, "House."

Myron leans his big bulky construction worker shoulder over me to get closer to the little page. "Oh, *howss*."

"Yeah. That's it. House. Like you live in."

"Sure."

"Good. Keep reading."

He dips his head down toward the page. "My—howss—is—red—and—white."

"Right! Myron, that's excellent!"

A smile cracks the weathered face. "T'anks, Ray."

"Okay. We have to stop, but you can take it home." I hand him the book. It's about twenty pages long. "Practice and we'll do it again in two weeks."

Myron stands, hiking his pants up by the leather work belt. "Okay." He takes *Where We Live: English for Beginners, Book One* in his big hand. "See you."

"Right, Myron. See you."

I follow him out of the rectory basement and into the parking lot of Our Lady of Czestochowa Church. OLC is what we call it. I do volunteer English tutoring here twice a month. I get service credit for school, but I'd do it even without that. It's cool to help the new people moving in. And it's a real charge teaching somebody to read!

We're greeted by music booming out of the little gray house across the street. It's a warm enough day that the windows are open. "Who stole the kishka? Who stole the kishka? Who stole the kishka? From the butcher's shop? Hey!"

It's Leon Bromiski's *Polka Time* radio show on WAWA. "Who Stole the Kishka" is a crack-up. It's basically about somebody stealing somebody else's sausage, which is what a *kishka* is. Not exactly hip music, but I've got to admit I get a kick out of it.

I make a left onto Bridgeton Pike. I feel like walking. I've got a lot of nervous energy. Tryouts are tomorrow. I mean, I'm ready, but I've got to make Malovic pick me. And last year, first time around, that didn't happen. Just thinking about it makes my stomach grab.

I've been working on my game, though. I went to the County CYO Basketball Camp this summer for a week and even though it wiped out half my summer savings, it was worth it. My J jelled for real that week. You shoot hundreds of jump shots when you're learning and you find yourself trying different things. Hold your hands this way. Hold this arm that way. Over and over, and then gradually, it's automatic pilot.

One of the coaches at camp described it and he was right on. He said, "The physics required to actually shoot this sphere through that hoop are incredible. You can't figure it out in your head or follow some kind of directions. Your body learns it."

I knew exactly what he meant. It leaves your hand, and you don't even have to look. You know when it's good. You know when it's off. By the feel. And then comes the best thing. When it goes in nice, when you let it flick off your fingers, it goes through the hoop and into the net and doesn't touch anything, and it is perfect and right there, and there's all that backspin, and the net goes piff.

It makes this little sound—*piff*. And the net kicks up at the end. Once I started getting that *piff* regular, I knew I had a solid J. I was still not a great ball handler, but most of the time I played forward at camp and didn't have to dribble much anyway.

"Who Stole the Kishka" and my happy camp memories bounce me along through Greenville. The town I live in is Franklin, but Greenville is what they call my neighborhood.

Down here by the church is the part of Greenville where the Polish immigrants live when they first come in. It's blocks and blocks of tight little brick row houses. My father says they all have the same plan. They work construction if they're guys, or clean houses if they're women.

They cram like ten people in an apartment, work at every job they can get, save their money, and then in a few years, if everything goes right, they get their own little Cape Cod like we have. My dad would know. It's what he did, and so did a lot of the guys who work for the construction company my dad and Uncle William started, C.P.G. Construction.

Which sounds like some international corporation. It's not. They have two trucks. C.P.G. stands for "Couple of Polish Guys."

My dad does have a sense of humor.

I keep walking till I get to the Farmers Market. It's a low, flat corrugated metal building with a concrete floor. I pull open the big double doors. It's like stepping into another world. The air is warm and moist and full of delicious aromas. Roasted peanuts. Pies. Apples. Those are the first stands. I walk in a bit and smell the rye bread, all yeasty and thick and hot, and the kielbasa with that garlic and spice filling the air. It floats right into my nose and down into my stomach.

The market is pretty empty now, late afternoon on a Tuesday, but on Saturday or Sunday, it's wall-to-wall people. I keep walking till I get to where all the poultry and egg stands are, and there's Walter at his family's little egg stand. Big neck. Big arms. Big blond, crew-cut head. Even big freckles.

Walter lives on an egg farm in North Franklin, but he's always been part of our neighborhood. His crazy cousin, Teddy Turkowski, lives around the corner from me, and Walter's parents would leave Walter there a lot so he'd have someone to play with besides chickens. That's how I got to know him. He even started coming to our school in second grade. His family must have been using the Turkowskis' address or something.

He's talking to a tiny old grandma in a dark coat and babushka. She's shaking her head. "I no can, Wal-ter. Is no good."

He pushes a carton of eggs at her. "Yeah, Mrs. K. No big deal."

She puts her hands up and backs away. "No. No."

"Here. Come on." He puts the carton in her handbasket, then pats her on the shoulder. "Right? We're okay. Pay me next time."

She makes these clucking noises, still shaking her head. "You good boy." She shuffles closer, makes him bend down so he's almost doubled over, and kisses him on the cheek.

Walter goes back to the stand and ducks under the counter. I walk over, deepen my voice, and talk like an old guy. "Hey, sonny, get me a dozen eggs, huh? And no cracked ones like last time!"

He pops up with his mouth open. Then he breaks out in that big grin of his. "Hey. My man! What's up?"

We slap hands. He's wearing his usual—dirty old jeans, big work boots, and a gray sweatshirt. "Nothing. I just finished over at the tutoring center. Figured I'd check you out before I went home."

"Cool. Hey, remember that time when I came with you and helped out?"

"Yeah. That one time. Then Father Bonzak bounced you."

Walter looks all disgusted. "That was lame. He wasn't into my innovative reading selections."

"*Maxim* and *Stuff* aren't generally considered good beginning English-as-a-second language material."

"Are you kidding? My guy was totally into it."

I crack up remembering. "That is true. He did learn a lot of new vocabulary." I reach over and run my hand along his buzz cut. "Why do you do that to your head? People are going to think you have lice."

"Hey, man. Don't knock my trendsetting hairdo." He brushes it up with his hands and some spit.

"Boys! What's going on?"

We turn around and there's Pruze. He comes strolling over, laces untied on his clunky skater shoes, long blond hair everywhere in his face.

Walter pounds a rhythm on the counter and chants real loud, "Pruze-a-kow-ski. Pruze-a-kow-ski." A dog a few stands down starts barking.

Pruze sways backs and forth to the beat and chants right back, "Wal-ter-Was-ko. Wal-ter-Was-ko."

The dog barks louder. I say, "Hey, you guys, knock it off. You're bugging the dog. She dislikes idiots."

Pruze's real name is Stan Pruzakowski. He moved here from Chicago this past summer. He's huge, he's funny, and he plays ball. In fact, he plays ball real well. There are now two ballplayers in Greenville. Me and Pruze. And I'm real happy for the company. We're both going out for the team.

Pruze leans on the counter. "So, what's up?"

Walter says, "Working my butt off like usual."

"Nothing. Just hangin' out," I say. "What's up with you?"

"I got to pick up some stuff for my mom." Pruze takes an egg out of one of the baskets and spins it on the counter. He nods at me. "Big day tomorrow, man."

Walter squints at me. "What big day?"

"B-ball tryouts tomorrow."

He snorts. "You're going out for Malovic again?"

I shrug. "What can I do? He's the man."

Walter reaches out real quick and snatches the baseball cap off my head. "Don't bother, that's what you can do." He puts my hat on his head. Backwards.

"Yeah, well . . ."

Walter shakes his head. "I still can't believe that jerk cut you last year."

My stomach automatically tightens at the word "cut."

"Yeah, don't sweat it." It's like I'm talking to myself.

Walter smiles and punches me lightly on the arm. "Hey. I know you're good. All I'm sayin' is, why waste your time? You're strong. Go out for wrestling. Stoshy is. Gerard. Macie. Paul. You guys'll kick butt."

The best wrestlers in the district are always from Greenville. It's like a tradition. Nobody up our way plays basketball for the school. To most guys in Greenville, basketball is a black guy's game. There are a couple of exceptions like me and Pruze, but we're definitely exceptions.

Pruze picks up a straw from under the table and throws it at Walter like a little spear. "Yeah, like you know all about it. C'mon, Ray. Let's go to your house and play some hoops. Let the Egg Man here talk trash to the chickens."

Walter shoots us a big grin. The freckles spread across his face. "I'm just goofin'. Lighten up. Look, I'm gonna give you my special good luck blessing."

Before I realize what he's doing, Walter takes an egg and cracks it open on my head! The cold goo slides down my hair. I yell, then grab Walter's shirt with one hand and an egg out of the basket with the other. He's pushing at me, but I manage to smash it on his chest. A big goopy hunk of it bounces off and splats on the floor.

Pruze backs off. "You boys are nuts!"

But Walter smears some of it on Pruze's chest before he can get away. Me, Pruze, and Walter are slapping around, cracking up, smearing egg on one another. The dog starts barking again. People are standing there staring at us. We're laughing like nuts.

Then somebody bellows, "*Stupid!*"

Next thing Walter comes pitching forward into me. My hat goes spinning off his head. We grab on to each other so we don't go down.

Walter's father is standing right behind him. He's a big guy. Like Walter, only more worn-out looking and heavy. His construction shirt looks like a tent. I can smell his sweat. And whiskey.

He pushes Walter again. Both hands thrust out hard. "You like to waste food?" Again. Push! "You like to waste money?"

Walter's eyes are bugging out. "No, Dad. I was just . . ."

"You think I dun watch what you're doing?"

Walter keeps backing up. "No, I mean—"

The dog starts barking again. Walter's father wheels around and yells, "Shut up your damn dog!"

A couple of old guys at the stand with the dog pet him and make him sit down. Walter's father turns back to Walter. "Clean it up! Now!"

Walter quick hustles behind the counter and comes back with a rag.

You've got to give Walter's father plenty of room, especially if he's had a few. Walter gets on his hands and knees and starts wiping the concrete.

One of the guys with the dog totters over to Walter's father. He puts a hand on his shoulder. "Hey, Michael. Take it easy. It's boys playing."

Walter's father shrugs him off. "You tell me what to do?" He spits on the ground and turns back to Walter. "Clean it up! I don't want to see a spot. Then you see me at the truck." He walks back through the big metal door behind their stand and outside. He slams it closed behind him.

Me and Pruze look at each other. The old guys shuffle

back to the stand, muttering and shaking their heads. I bend over to Walter. "Gimme a rag, man. I'll help."

Pruze says, "Yeah. Where are the rags at?"

Walter doesn't look up. "This is nothing. Go ahead. I'll catch you tomorrow."

"You sure?" I glance toward the door. I want to make sure his dad is still outside. "You wanna come with us?"

He talks to the floor. "Nah. In five minutes he'll be sleeping it off. You better go."

Pruze says, "All right. See ya."

I pat him on the back. "Yeah. See ya, man."

Walter doesn't say anything else. Just keeps scrubbing at the concrete even though all that's left is a little dark stain.

chapter two
COMMITTED TO THE TEAM

When I walk into the cafeteria the next morning, Walter is slumped over our usual table. He's got his tractor cap pulled down way low over his face. Walter gets to school first off the early bus. There's maybe another fifty kids or so scattered around at tables.

He peers up at me from under the cap. "Hey."

"Hey." I flop down in the seat across from him.

"You see Macie's new wheels?" Walter nods toward the parking lot at a beautiful metallic blue car. "That's a '92 'Vette."

"Yeah. I saw it all weekend. He hasn't stopped cruising it since he got it Friday night."

Walter stretches his big arms out and yawns all loud and crazy. Two girls at the next table spin around to see if an animal is being tortured. Walter shoots them a grin. "Wish I had something like that instead of a truck I can only drive after school."

"At least you got wheels," I say. "All I've got is feet."

He chuckles. "You wanna go fishing later over at the lake? I've got an hour after school before I have to be at the stand."

"No, man. I've got b-ball."

He shakes his head. "I forgot. You're really doin' that again?"

"Today's the day." I try to sound nonchalant, but I couldn't even eat this morning.

Walter just shakes his head. I look at his feet. The usual big, mud-caked clodhoppers. I'm not sure I should bring it up, but I do. "How'd you make out with your old man yesterday?"

Walter stares out the window at Macie's 'Vette. "Same old thing. He yells for a while. Then he falls asleep." He sounds bored.

"Serious. Everything's cool?"

The grin is fixed in place. "Like a cucumber."

He's obviously done talking about it. It's got to be embarrassing as hell to have your father drunk and pushing you around in front of people.

Not to mention scary.

The bell rings. I hop up. Walter slides out of his chair, and we walk into the hall together. He leans on me. "Remember you shoot the ball through the hoop. Don't try to kick it in. Better yet, blow it off and go fishing."

"Thanks. Advice from an expert. And with that pencil, remember to use the pointy end."

He raps me on the skull with his knuckles and runs off grinning. We head to our classes. At least I go to mine. Walter's attendance is not known to be absolutely perfect.

I'm sitting on the bench in the locker room tying and untying my sneakers trying to get them just right. Tight enough so they are like a part of my foot, but not so tight that I lose the feeling in my feet. This year the announcement said there's going to be two days of tryouts. The thing with tryouts is you don't *kind of* make a team. You're on or you're off. And there's one guy who makes that decision—Malovic.

Pruze walks by, bends over, and with one quick move, opens the lace I just got perfect.

"Hey!" I slap at his hand and bounce up off the bench after him.

He laughs. "I'm loosening you up, man. Get it?"

I chase him out onto the court. He jogs down toward Ziggy, whose moon face cracks into a smile when he sees us. A second later Richie D joins us. We are it.

The little white corner.

I try to stay calm and think rationally about this. With my J becoming so automatic, my defense real tight, and my rebounding strong, I'm not the same player Malovic saw last year. Plus Pruze is here with me this year. I don't know how that's going to help, but I'm glad he's here anyway.

I slide under the basket looking for a rebound. Tyrone Hayes is next to me. He's an awesome senior. He can dunk, he can shoot outside, he's got a hook. He's huge, with big shoulders and hands. Just awesome.

I sneak a peek at Tyrone when a whistle blows. Everybody turns. Malovic is standing on the side wearing his same gray sweats. Right away all his old boys, Robert, Gel Head, all that crew, run over and practically hug him. They're smiling and jabbering away. I've got to remember—I'm good. I did great in camp.

When we start off with line backs, I line up as close to where Malovic is as I can. Robert comes over and lines up right next to me. He's wearing these silky red basketball shorts with black trim. There's a number 10 on them. He still has part of his uniform from last year! Nobody in any sport gets to keep any part of the uniform from school. But somehow Robert gets to keep his game shorts.

I run like a dog, trying to beat everybody, and I pretty much do. Except for Robert. Robert is just quick. No two ways about it.

When we go to shoot jumpers, I get on the side where Malovic is. On my first go-round in the drill, me, the Gel Head kid, and Robert are all in this one line. I pop mine first. Gel Head follows and hits his. Then Robert hits one. Three in a row. Which is cool, because you try to get your line to get the most and you call out the numbers as you make them.

As we jog to the back of our line, Malovic nods. "Nice hit, Rudy. Nice shot, Robert."

Now, I know he saw me hit mine. But he says nothing to

me about it. Do I have to introduce myself? "Hi, I'm Ray. I hit my jumper too?"

My ballhandling drills are still not pretty, but I manage to make sure I don't get matched up with Robert, and I try to get as far away from Malovic as I can on that one.

Then we break into squads to run the scrimmages. I figure at this point I'm doing good. My shots are dropping. I rebounded good in the drills. Was one of the fastest out there. Only the dribbling was on the downside.

I get on, but nobody's giving me the ball. I'm running my jewels off going back and forth with nothing happening. Just like last year. Finally, I get the ball off a rebound and who matches up on me? My favorite guy—Robert.

He's harassing me, reaching in and trying to knock the ball away. Guys are yelling for me to pass, but I'm going to the hoop this time. I've got to show Malovic what I can do. That I can take Robert.

Robert uses his hand to give me a little shove on the hip, but I keep coming. He lays his body on me and I pound the ball up the floor, lower my shoulder, lean into him, and go ramming forward to the basket for a layup. His leg gets in between mine, and I lose my balance. We thump to the floor in a heap. The ball skips out-of-bounds.

"Wrong wit' you!" Robert grunts. He bounces up, his face contorted.

I jump up too. Malovic blows the whistle. He signals at me and stares hard through his glasses. "Offensive foul."

Offensive foul! He was pushing me the whole way! That's what I'd like to say.

Gel Head Rudy mouths off, "Damn straight. Boy can't even walk right. He's dangerous. Get him off the floor."

This kid is really looking for it.

For the second day of tryouts, as soon as I hit the locker room, I do the self-talk. Got to do it. I can do it. I feel a rhythm building inside me. Almost like a beat. It's some kind of last chance desperate energy. I am totally focused. I feel it during warm-ups. Go up, flick the wrist, *piff*! Hit the shot! Go up, flick the wrist, *piff*! Hit the shot. I *will* show Malovic.

I am hot in all the drills. I pick up every loose ball near me. Every ball is *my* ball. I am even banging under the boards taking rebounds away from Pruze. "Whoa, man. You're on fire," he says.

When the scrimmages start, first time down I get open on the wing, right in front of Malovic, and Pruze passes it back out to me. I don't hesitate. I take it, go straight up. *Piff!* Right there. On defense I match up with Rudy. I learned to play some tight D in camp. There was a coach there we called Spider. He was this long-armed guy who was big into defense. He showed me how to position myself and to really get into playing D.

"Watch his stomach, Ray. Where his stomach goes that's where he's going to go. Don't fall for any other stuff: head, eyes, feet. That's all junk. Watch their belly." And he was right. It worked. Spider started calling me The Stopper. If someone would start scoring, Spider would rap me on the shoulder and say, "Switch. Stopper, you're on him."

In the scrimmage I hold Rudy to nothing. I hit two more Js and that feels real good and gets me up and excited. I'm playing like I played in camp. Then, right at the whistle, I hit a three that swishes—*piff!*

As we're coming off the court for the next five to go on, Malovic calls to us, "Good job."

We finish with sprints, and I'm right there at the front of the pack. Me and Robert, of course.

At the end of the session Powell is walking around asking for shoe sizes. He goes over to Pruze right away. Then Robert. I wait right where I am. Come on, Powell. He goes to Ziggy. Tyrone. This time I know he's coming to me. I just ran nine straight points, grabbed five rebounds, and shut down my man on defense, all against varsity guys.

Powell keeps walking around. I'm at the end of the alphabet so I'll probably be last. I just keep shooting. He goes to Rudy. C'mon over here, Powell.

Then he hands the clipboard to Malovic.

I want to walk over, grab the clipboard, and smash it in two.

The same guys who were doing it last year with Malovic head up to the bleachers again. On his way up, Rudy strolls by me all casual and says, "There ya go."

Me and the other cuts sit in the middle so *the team* can

all look down on us. Malovic gives his cut speech. Everybody gets a fair shot, blah, blah, blah. Fair shot my butt. Richie D leans over and whispers, "Screw it. I'm not goin' through this bull again next year."

I nod. At the end of the speech I get up and head for the locker room. I feel like crying or hitting somebody or something. I don't know if I'm going to do this again either.

Then Malovic calls out, "Roy."

A couple of us turn around. There is no Roy. He's looking at me. "Roy? Can I see you?"

I answer slowly. "Me? I'm Ray." Hold on. He made a mistake. He forgot to call me up to the bleachers. I'm getting on at the last possible second!

He smiles at me. He lowers his voice so we're having a private conversation. "Right. I'm sorry—Ray. I understand you've kept the book in the PAL league on occasion."

"Yeah, a couple of times." What does that have to do with anything?

"How about working with our team this year as one of our managers and scorekeepers?" He's looking real earnest with his beaky nose right in my face.

This is not good. I don't want to be a scorer or a manager at all. I mumble something because he's standing there waiting. "I don't know. I hadn't thought about it."

He talks real steady. "Well, you were going to make a commitment to the team when you tried out. You can still make that commitment, just in a different capacity, right?"

I look around. He's waiting for an answer. "I . . . I guess."

He smiles real big. Then he actually puts a hand on my shoulder. "What do you say there, Ray? Are you our new manager?"

chapter three
THAT B-BALL CRAP

I need time to think. I stumble around looking for words. "I don't know. I think . . . I mean, I've got to check."

He glances back at the guys on the bleachers who are starting to cut up. "Well, think about it. Let me know tomorrow, either way. Stop at my office before school."

He smiles and nods at me, letting me know we're done. "Okay. Uh, thanks." I nod and walk backwards toward the locker room again.

I go in there and guys are throwing things around and banging lockers. Not a lot of talking, but lots of banging. I sit down on the bench and loosen my sneakers. I feel kind of jumpy. Full of energy and nothing to do with it.

I throw my street clothes into my gym bag, pull on my sweats, and head out into the hall. I look at my watch. Walter is probably still waiting for his bus. I jog on down there. He's leaning against the wall under the bus port. When he sees me, he snaps to attention and salutes.

"Here he comes. Basketball team captain!"

I walk over. "Not quite."

"So?"

I spit on the ground. "Crap."

He leans back against the wall. "Could have told you this was gonna happen."

"Yeah, you're a real psychic."

"Don't have to be a psychic with Malovic. I don't get why you want to run around with all these rugheads anyway."

I automatically sneak a look around. One of these days he's going to say something like that and some big black dude is going to be right there. There's a lot of people I know talk like that, though. Even my mother. She won't say something like "rughead," but she'll speak in this code, saying stuff to my aunt like, "There was a lot of dark clouds when I went shopping today." It's not a big deal, but it rubs me the wrong way.

I got no problem with black people. I mean, I got nothing much to do with them either, except for trying to get on the basketball team. Nobody in Greenville is black. I didn't even have a black kid in my class till seventh grade, when we got to the middle school. And at school they pretty much do their thing and we do ours. No problem.

It's quiet for a couple of seconds. Then I figure I'll tell Walter. "Well, he did offer me a place on the team."

"How's that?"

I put my gym bag down. "He wants me to be a score-keeper and manager."

Walter laughs. "Oh yeah, you could be the ball boy. What a great offer."

I move my bag around with my foot. "I don't know. Maybe if he gets to know me, I'll have a better shot next year."

He shakes his head. "No, man, it's like this: You be score-keeper and you do a good job, you know what that'll get you? Scorekeeper's job next year. I'm telling you, Ray. You ain't his kind of player. And we both know what kind that is."

"Pruze made it."

"No duh. He's from some damn Chicago ghetto."

"Ziggy too."

"Two white guys. Big whoop. Bet that pinhead Robert made it."

That was a surprise. "*You* know Robert?"

"Oh yeah. That moron-pain-in-the-butt. He's in all my dumbo classes." Walter bounces off the wall. "Ray. I *know* Malovic. He's my guidance counselor." Walter spits. "If you're black, you can be as dumb as a post and always in trouble, like your pal Robert, and with Malovic, you're an American Idol."

I snort. "Yeah, whatever."

He points at me. "You don't think so, huh? Pruze says you're better than half the guys on the team." He lifts his eye-brows. "So, why did Malovic keep guys who are just as good as you, but give you the ax? And what kind of guys did he keep?"

I shake my head. I don't have a good answer.

That night I'm in bed staring at the ceiling. I feel like a jerk feeling sorry for myself. Plenty of people have a lot worse problems. I can still play ball with the Falcons. Maybe I should just forget about school ball. But if I were to become scorekeeper, Malovic might think real seriously about putting me on next year. In the meantime, though, I would look like a dweeb.

I don't sleep well.

The next day I start down to Malovic's office before first period. I'm still going back and forth in my head about keeping the book and I'm almost there. I've got to tell him something.

Then as I walk up the front hall to the office, I have a revelation: What if someone gets injured during the season? Guys get injured all the time. Malovic would already be liking me for helping out with the book and everything, and then—bam! He could put me in. I'd be right there.

I put my hand on the side door rail. I'm not real proud of this, but it could be my way onto the team.

Malovic's office is a tight, little paneled room, gray metal desk, shelves full of binders, and walls lined with file cabinets. The door is open and Malovic is sitting at his desk writing something, so I knock. I'm going to do it. I'm going to say yes. I put on a smile.

He doesn't look up. "Come in."

I'm going to do it. I say, "Hi, Mr. Malovic."

He looks up. A big smile creases his face. "Ray! Hi! Come on in."

I'm going to do it. I take two steps into the room and freeze when I see somebody in the far corner by the window. It's Robert, leaning on a file cabinet, eating something.

"Ray." Malovic gestures at a chair. "It's good to see you. Sit down."

"Yeah. Thanks." I try to keep my eyes on Malovic, but it's hard not to check Robert out.

Malovic turns and looks over his shoulder at Robert. "Robert, Ray is thinking about joining us on the team as manager this year."

A slow grin creeps over Robert's face. Malovic turns back to me. Meanwhile, Robert doesn't say a thing, but shakes his head very slightly, real slow from side to side. I can read the message: "You pitiful punk. You can't play with guys as good as me so you're going to keep track of our points."

Robert takes a sloppy bite of a big old powdered doughnut. He's wearing this black turtleneck sweater and he's got white powder all over the front. He's standing around in a guidance counselor's office eating a doughnut like he owns the place and shaking his head about me.

Malovic says, "Well, Robert. I'll see you later. I have to talk to Ray right now."

Robert walks slowly around the desk to the door. I give him a nod and say hey to be polite, in front of Malovic.

Robert doesn't even bother to look. Doesn't say anything to me or Malovic, just slides out right past me almost bumping me, his head bobbing along real cool, eating his doughnut like a slob. I do a one-eighty right there. The little jerk. No way am I going to keep score for him.

Malovic leans back in his chair with his hands behind his head. All relaxed. Real upbeat he says, "So. You're going to help us out this year, Raymond?"

I hate the way he puts it. It's like I would have to say, "No, I don't want to help you out." Instead I mumble, "I just came to tell you that I, uh, can't do it this year. Sorry."

I'm ready to leave now. I said my bit. But he leans forward. "Why's that, Ray?"

I didn't know he would ask questions! What can I say? I can't be your scorekeeper because I'm not going to hand out water bottles and towels and count points for a stuck-up chump like Robert? I finally look at the top of his desk and say, "Just don't really want to do that." Which is pretty much the truth.

He looks at me and then all of a sudden has to move some papers around. He lets out this little sigh. "Okay, Ray. I knew you wanted to be involved with the team and I thought I would give you a chance. Thanks for stopping in." There's still a smile on his face, but not in his voice anymore.

I get up out of the chair and slide to the door. "Okay, thanks. Bye."

My heart is thumping as I walk back down the hall. I just

threw away a great chance. But I had to do it. I couldn't make myself be a slave to guys like Robert or Rudy after that little taste of what was to come, no matter what the upside might have been.

That night me, Walter, Stoshy, and Gerard hang out at my house. It feels good to have my friends around after this morning. We go down to the basement and watch some Dr. Shock. When we get together on a Friday night, we always have to watch *Dr. Shock* on The Scream Channel. Dr. Shock is this guy who dresses up in a cheap-looking vampire suit and makes stupid jokes during the commercial breaks in all these old horror movies like *The Wolf Man* and *Frankenstein*. They're fun to watch and Walter goes ape over them, cheering the monsters on. We're waiting for Walter when the show starts.

Gerard points at the screen. "Look, doesn't the Creature from the Black Lagoon look like Jeanine Pieslak?"

Stoshy howls. "Oh man. You're still sweet on her."

Gerard and Stoshy look almost like twins. Small, strong guys with short blond hair and big noses. Kind of like Barney Rubble. Gerard smacks the back of Stoshy's head with a *TV Guide*. "Get out of here!"

"I saw you dancing with her at the OLC Christmas party. You were getting all emotional."

"She stepped on my pinky toe with those damn chunky shoes. Broke my toe!"

"How *are* things on the girl front?" I ask.

They both give a thumbs-down. Gerard says, "How about you?"

"Nothing." I'm in the same boat. I haven't had a serious involvement with a girl since Theresa Micinski in ninth grade. She and I kissed twice at a party, so in my wild and crazy social set we were considered an item for about half a year.

Unfortunately, I don't think we're going to make a lot of inroads with girls hanging out watching *Dr. Shock*. I tell the boys what went down with Malovic's offer.

Stoshy listens shaking his head, then says, "Forget basketball. We still need somebody to wrestle at a hundred and sixty pounds. I could talk to Coach Downs. It's not too late."

Stoshy's been on the wrestling team for two years now. So has Gerard. Walter thumps down the steps. "Hey, sweethearts! What's going on?"

Gerard says, "Don't bother Ray-Ray. He's having a bad Malovic Day."

Walter points at me. "Did you go be his ball boy?"

I shake my head. "No. I couldn't handle it."

Walter grabs a big pawful of pretzels out of the bowl. "Thank goodness. You would have looked like a real dipstick."

Stoshy, his mouth full of popcorn, says, "That's what I just told him."

Walter flops on the old plaid sofa. He says, "Forget about

it, Ray. Be a real Greenville boy. Get out there and wrestle! You don't need that b-ball crap."

Gerard and Stoshy are nodding. But they're all three wrong.

I do need that b-ball crap.

chapter four
ROCK

I don't go out for wrestling. All year I keep playing ball. It's like an ache if I don't. I play for the Falcons on Saturdays and for this school service club I belong to, the Key Club, on Wednesday nights. I go to the varsity games and watch Pruze. And I shoot on my hoop every morning and night.

Now that it's summer I immediately start working for my uncle Jerzy doing landscaping, which means pulling weeds and cutting grass at office complexes. My dad can't hire me because he says he's got grown men with families waiting on him for a job. When the weather's decent, Walter and I do some fishing at the lake. Usually around dinner, when Walter's father sometimes lets him leave the stand for an hour.

The lake is only two blocks from my house. It's not much. Kind of small and muddy, with a soury smell like old leaves rotting. You definitely don't swim in it. The parents all think it's a big deal that we have a lake in the neighborhood. Like we're in the country or something. They love to sit out at night on lawn chairs and look at it, till the mosquitoes chase them in.

Me, Walter, and some of the other guys hang there, too, sometimes. Warm weather and no school always brings everybody in the neighborhood out. After my first day on the job I take a walk down to the lake after dinner.

My father and mother have their chairs up on the grass by the picnic tables. They look kind of alike from the back. Big, stocky, strong, with short white hair. Peasant stock, my dad always says. Walter, Stoshy, and Gerard are already sitting on the rocks by the water.

I wander down. "Hey, what's up?"

Walter throws a pebble at me. "Lawn boy!"

I grab a rock and have a seat. "What's goin' on?"

Stoshy says, "How's work?"

"Hot."

Stoshy is painting for his father. Walter is working his tail off over at the farm and the Farmers Market. Days *and* nights. Gerard has got it easy. He's stocking shelves at CVS. Inside. Air-conditioning. Girl clerks.

Gerard says, "Hey, you all want to go to Bridgeton tomorrow night? They're showing *Night of the Living Dead* at that place that shows all the old movies."

I shake my head. "Can't. I've got an SAT prep class." That was something I knew I better do this summer. It's only one night a week anyway.

Walter says, "For what?"

I hit him with a pebble. "To do good on the SATs, duh."

Stoshy says, "I'm goin' to CCC. You don't need SATs or anything."

CCC is our local community college. Colonial County College. Gerard chimes in, "Me too. It's free. Or just about."

Stoshy skips a stone. "Are you still thinking about going to State?"

"Yeah. I'm going to apply there and some other schools." My grades are good enough, I just need to make sure my SATs are up there. Mr. Pinto, my guidance counselor, said they have a great teacher education program.

Walter looks at me and squints. "You don't want to go too far, big boy." He bounces another pebble at me. "You'll need us to help show you how to drink beer and other college stuff like that."

Stoshy laughs. "Yeah, like the women!"

I stretch my arms out. "I'm sure I can handle it."

"Walter!"

Walter jumps up in one motion. "Shit."

It's Walter's father up by my parents. He's yelling down. "Move it!"

Walter jogs up the bank. Over his shoulder he calls back, "There's the work whistle. Later."

We all yell, "Yeah. Later."

Walter and his father disappear down the street to their truck. You got to wonder how Walter turned out to be such a cool, funny guy with an old man like that.

Gerard says, "You wanna watch TV over at my house? Yankees are on."

Stoshy nods. "Yeah. C'mon, Ray."

They both get up so I do too. "Nah. I'm going to shoot some hoop." My father always says it's better to be playing a sport instead of watching someone else playing it. I got to agree.

We go up to the street and split. I go into my garage and get my ball out and start shooting. After about ten minutes, Pruze comes walking by. He's got on stringy cutoff shorts and a dirty old white T-shirt with a picture of Snoopy on it. The only thing sharp on him are his basketball shoes. "Hey, Ray. What's going on?"

I toss him the ball as he comes up the driveway. He takes it and swishes it from the corner. Pruze is big and he's heavy-duty. A little too heavy, actually, but he's solid. He's a tough guy under the boards. He was the only white starter this year.

I rebound it, take the ball back, do some stutter steps, go right up and lay it in.

"We could have used you this year, Ray." He takes the rebound and shoots again from the same spot. It just drops right down and in. *Piff!*

The ball rolls back to him. He shakes the hair out of his face, fires me a pass on the run, and I scoop it up, sky to the hoop, and lay it down real gentle and in.

"See, Ray. You can get up. You can shoot. And you play D."

"Yeah." It's nice to hear Pruze talking like this.

"You should play ROCK this summer."

ROCK stands for Recreation, Opportunity, Challenge, Knowledge. It's this county program that's supposed to "uplift" the area youth by having them play basketball and go to picnics and dances and stuff. Real logical.

Most all of the ROCK stuff I've seen advertised is in Jefferson Park, the black section of town. The different neighborhoods in Franklin are just that—different. You got all us Polacks in Greenville in the south end. On the east side—it's Jefferson Park. On the north end is Regent's Park, where the rich kids live. Rich like two-Volvos-in-the-drive-way-in-front-of-the-three-car-garage rich. A little farther north are the last few farms.

Nobody I know has ever done a ROCK thing. I pass the ball to Pruze. "You goin' to?"

"Yeah, man. You just get a form down at town hall. It's twenty bucks to play. They put you on a team and it's two nights a week during all of July. There's some college dudes who are like player-coaches and it's all high school guys playing. You should definitely do it."

I know ROCK being kind of a black thing doesn't faze Pruze. I guess he was used to that in Chicago. I've even seen him cruising with this older guy on the team, Tommy Chessman. He's this black dude who has to duck to go through doorways because he's almost seven feet tall. I bounce a pass back to Pruze again.

"I don't know."

Pruze puts the ball under his arm and walks over to me. "Look, Ray. Do you know who runs the ROCK league?"

"Who?"

"Malovic."

I roll my eyes. "Oh, now I can't wait to sign up."

Pruze starts dribbling. "You ever want to make it on the school team you got to show him you got a game against varsity guys." He snaps a pass to me.

I hold the ball. "I did show him."

"Well, obviously not enough to suit him."

I shoot a bank shot, rebound it, and jump high to roll it on over the rim. "I don't know."

"What don't you know? It'll be like a month-long try-out in front of Malovic. Anyway, you gotta get in there with these varsity guys and get some experience playing on their level. You ain't gonna get it with the pitiful Bridgeton Falcons. Capisce?"

Pruze has got me. He knows if it really gets me closer to making the team, I've got to go for it. "Yeah. I guess."

"Cool. Maybe we'll get on the same team." He takes a jumper and swishes it.

"Yeah."

I pass him the ball. He dunks it. He passes back to me. I swish it from twenty. I get a quick picture in my head of me and Pruze tearing up the league together. But I have to wonder. Can I handle ROCK?

Pruze says, "Oh my god. Hold me up." He's staring down the street.

I follow his gaze. It's Stacey Steck. She's wearing a tank top and these tiny denim shorts. She is tan. She smiles real big and waves. "Hi, guys!"

I nod and force a word out of my semi-paralyzed mouth. "Stacey."

Stacey's got coppery red hair, green eyes, and a dynamite figure. She used to be Stacey Steckanovich till her parents changed their name. She is the ultimate: smart, good-looking, class president, everything. Unbelievably she lives in our neighborhood and has been in school with me since kindergarten, but she might as well be on another planet. I'm a regular person. She is not.

Pruze slaps himself in the forehead and says, "Is it time for our date already? I forgot. I am *so* sorry."

Stacey laughs as she strolls on by. "Well, Stanley. I'm not sure your attire is entirely appropriate for my standard of dating."

Pruze keeps staring. "Well, yours is good for my standard!"

She laughs again. "Right. See ya, guys."

"Bye." We both just have to watch her all the way to the corner.

A week after I send in my twenty bucks and my ROCK registration form, I get a call. I'm out in the driveway shooting after dinner. I pick it up in the kitchen. "Hello?"

"This Ray?" It's a black guy. I never got a phone call from a black guy before.

"Yeah."

"This is Tyrone Hayes. You on my ROCK team, man. We got a game Friday at seven o'clock at the middle school."

"Okay. I'll be there. Thanks."

"Okay." And he hangs up.

Giant Tyrone. He just graduated. He's the biggest and best player ever to come out of the high school. I think about playing on Tyrone's team, and I hope I'm good enough. Second, I hope I'm not the only white guy.

Two nights later, I show up at the middle school gym. It's steaming out. You can see it around the streetlights. Like a halo of haze. All the doors to the gym are propped wide open, and I can hear balls bouncing and sneakers squeaking on the wood floor, even from the parking lot.

A big blue banner over the door says ROCK YOUR SUMMER in bright yellow letters. I walk in and look around for Tyrone. He's standing with a bunch of guys, all wearing red jerseys that say TRAMMEL INSURANCE in white letters on the front. He's talking real loud and the guys are laughing. I walk toward the group till I notice a shiny black head in the middle of the pack. Robert. I slow down. Right next to him is Rudy Kazootie with that stupid gelled hairdo of his. Why am I so lucky?

I go over and stand around on the outside of the little

circle. I don't want to interrupt the story or whatever. Jamal and Al Hayes are in the circle, too. I've seen them all play on varsity. They're Tyrone's brothers. Jamal graduated already and Al is my year. They're both over six three. Jamal is built like a monster. He's got big heavy brows and a huge chest and arms. Al is leaner, but also strong-looking. All three are excellent players.

Then out of the locker room comes Malovic. ROCK is looking like a real fun time now with Malovic *and* Robert *and* Rudy. He blows a whistle and calls out, "All right. First game. Insurance and Auto Glass. Get your fives on the floor."

Tyrone, Al, Jamal, Rudy, and Robert head out onto the court. Two other black guys sit down on the bench. They're both younger. I've seen them around, but don't know who they are. Next thing you know, the game starts, so I take a seat on the bench.

Malovic is reffing. Running back and forth. The teams are pretty even. I see a lot of guys from varsity and JV. Tyrone is skying and dunking and looking real strong. After a while Malovic blows the whistle and says, "Quarter!"

Our guys come and sit down on the bench, wiping off with towels and guzzling out of water bottles. I figure I better let Tyrone know I'm here at least. I walk over to the huddle and he's talking a mile a minute. "Jamal, man, you go low post, then come up at me. We set the double pick at the top for Robert. He can go down the side or dish to us."

Malovic blows the whistle. "Let's go! Second quarter."

I tap Tyrone lightly on the shoulder. He doesn't feel it. He walks out onto the court and away from me. I follow him. "Hey, Tyrone."

He's still walking. I have to get a little louder. "Hey, Tyrone!"

He turns and looks at me like I just came out of a flying saucer. He doesn't say anything.

"I'm Ray. We talked on the phone."

He just keeps looking.

"I'm on your team."

Then with the same blank expression he says, "Yeah. Okay. We talk at the half." And he turns and goes to the center to jump.

I feel pretty stupid standing there halfway out on the court. It's obvious to anybody watching that I was just basically told to sit down and stay out of the way, but there's not a lot to do about it—except sit down.

The second quarter goes pretty much like the first—even up—but Robert is shooting really crazy stuff from everywhere now. When the whistle blows for the half, I check the scoreboard. We're behind five points. Walking off the court, Tyrone is yelling at Robert, "What are you, stupid, man?"

Robert doesn't look at him. Tyrone points a long finger at Robert's chest. "You better do what I'm telling you, or you'll be sitting. I don't have to put up with your BS."

Robert just walks over to the water fountain. Tyrone watches with a sour look. He chugs from his sport bottle. I go over and give him a friendly "hey."

He wheels around almost yelling, "What!"

I try to stay steady and not let my voice shake. "You got a jersey for me?"

He studies me for a second. "Yeah. In the bag." He points at this gym bag in the third row. Then he goes back to drinking.

I reach in and there's one jersey left—number 2, which is nobody's number I've ever heard of. I strip off my T-shirt and put on the jersey. It hangs down almost to my knees. I tuck it in and that helps a little, but everybody else is wearing theirs out, so I pull it out again.

Malovic blows the whistle. "One minute," he yells. He walks over to Tyrone. "Tyrone. Reminder. Everybody plays a quarter."

Tyrone says, "Yeah. I know. Thanks."

I stand near Tyrone. The other guys look me over. Now that I've got a jersey on, they all realize I'm on the team. Tyrone looks from face to face and yells, "No more crap! I wanna win this game. These guys are nuthin'. They're nuthin'!" He slams the bench with his fist.

One of the two young guys whines, "Hey, man, we ain't played yet. When you gonna play us?"

Tyrone looks like he got a sudden headache. His forehead is all wrinkled. "All right. Larry, you go in for Al. Fred, you in for Rudy."

Rudy says, "Aw, man. How we gonna win with these lamos out there?"

Tyrone snaps at him, "This is league rules. They got to play."

Fred and Larry slap hands and walk out onto the court. I go back and sit. The third quarter starts. After about five minutes, Tyrone subs the two young guys out and puts Rudy and Al back in. They're moaning and groaning, but no one's paying attention. The quarter ends and Auto Glass leads by two.

Everybody comes off the floor dripping sweat like crazy. I get up and go over. This is my quarter. I lean into the huddle. Tyrone is yelling, "You guys got to work the ball! Robert, you throwin' up nonsense. Pass the ball!"

"Yeah." Robert barely talks.

"Don't 'yeah' me, just do what I'm tellin' you! Okay, this quarter, I'm gonna draw their zone in and hit you guys outside. Robert, you and Rudy stay top and work the ball and play some defense. You doin' nothin' on D!"

Robert just looks away. Malovic blows the whistle. "Fourth quarter. Let's go."

All the same guys walk out onto the court. They're going back out without me. I jog up next to Tyrone. "Hey, I'm in this quarter. Right?"

Tyrone says kind of low, "You play next game. This one too close."

"But . . ."

The whistle blows again. He gives me an annoyed look. "Just sit down, man." Then he turns and starts walking out onto the court.

chapter five
FOUR POINTS

All my fear of Tyrone goes right out the window. The anger rubs that out. I step in front of him. "I'm supposed to play this quarter."

He stares at me like I'm crazy. Malovic calls over, "Let's go."

I say pretty loud, "I'm in this quarter, right, Tyrone? I didn't play yet, so this must be my quarter."

Tyrone looks annoyed, but Malovic is watching him. "Uh, yeah. Rudy, you sit."

Rudy screams in this high-pitched voice, "What! I know this lamo white boy! He can't play!"

"You sit, we got league rules."

"This is BS."

Tyrone barks, "Shut up and sit down!"

Rudy flops down on the bleachers and throws a towel over his head. I walk on. The Auto Glass center, this big, heavy guy called Curly, says, "Uh-oh. He bringin' out the big gun for the last quarter."

Everybody laughs except Tyrone, Al, and Jamal. Tyrone gives me an evil look. He points at the guy Rudy was covering and says, "You play him. And play him good!"

He's a little guard with real smooth skin and cornrows. They call him Winnie. Winston is his real name. I've seen him on the varsity team. He gets the ball off the tap and tries to move on me, but I'm in his way and put a hand on his back. He snarls, "Get off," and pushes at my hand. I stay right with him and put the hand back on. You're allowed a hand as long as you don't push with it or get caught pushing with it.

He has to pass off. He hits his forward on the wing. The forward goes right by Robert, pulls up short, and floats a jumper for an easy two.

We charge down the other way. Al brings it up and hits Tyrone with a nice pass. Tyrone cuts across the middle and lays it in. We go back and forth a few times and go up two points, now that Al and Jamal and Tyrone have their passing thing going.

Then I get a pass from Al back to me at the top. It surprises me. I put up a quick jumper, but Curly comes across and blocks it so hard it slams against the bleachers. The whole gym goes, "Ooooooh." I feel stupid. I shouldn't have rushed the shot. Curly is slapping high fives with his guys. Big deal. Still our ball.

Tyrone calls out, "Substitution." He points at me. "You sit. Rudy, you on."

I've played maybe two minutes! Even though I'm embarrassed by the shot, I'm not putting up with that junk, even from a giant like Tyrone. "Wait a minute. I'm supposed to play a quarter."

Tyrone talks through gritted teeth. "You just played the quarter."

I am still in my stubborn mode. Tyrone is big, but I figure, what's he going to do? Kill me here in front of everyone? I hold his stare and keep my voice steady. "I played maybe two minutes *of* the quarter."

Tyrone walks up and towers over me. He hisses, "Sit your butt down."

That shakes me a little. He's some big guy, but I'm not sitting down. I came here tonight to play. I deserve to play the quarter. Malovic comes over. "What's the holdup here?"

My voice is getting stronger now. "Mr. Malovic, when you say we're supposed to play a quarter, you mean a full quarter, right?"

He looks at me, and I can see he is not happy. I've had my two minutes and that's all someone like me, not one of the real players in his book, is supposed to get. He gets his face back together and looks at Tyrone and says, "Right. Full quarter. League rules."

Tyrone looks like he ate a lemon. "Rudy, sit."

Rudy actually stamps his feet like a toddler. "Man!" He glares at me. "I'm gonna get you, punk."

"Yeah." I'm definitely not scared of Rudy. In fact, I'm real bugged at this point with all this crap.

Malovic looks at his watch. "Let's go. We have another game after this one." We set up quick. Tyrone throws it in to Robert and Robert hits a quick jumper. I see Rudy leaving the gym, going out the door. That's how much he cares about the team.

I D up hard on Winnie. I front him, denying him the ball. Their big guys keep trying to kick out to him anyway. Finally they try one time too many and I deflect it to Tyrone who throws it to Al on the run. Al goes up and bangs it home. We're up two.

I look at the clock. Six minutes left. On offense I run on the wings. I still don't see the ball and the Auto Glass guys start sagging off of me, so they can double-team the other guys. Al picks up on this and passes it over. I love shooting from an angle where I can bank it in. I go up, smooth, straight, release, bang, swish, two!

I trot back. Al says, "Nice buss."

"Nice pass," I say. I scored in ROCK! We're up four.

They miss. We go down again. They sag and start double-teaming Tyrone. He spots me standing there on the wing. He looks to Robert, but Robert is covered tight by Winnie. Tyrone finally throws it to me.

I catch it, don't think, just go straight up. Release. *Piff!* Another two.

We're up six. Then I hear this loud voice, "Go, Ray!" I have to look and there's Pruze sitting on our bench.

There's only about two minutes left. We D up strong and

they lose it out-of-bounds. They're yelling at one another. Robert picks it up and throws it in quick while they're still arguing and he hits Al on the fly. Al passes to Jamal, to Tyrone on the trailer, who stuffs it home. The Hayes brothers sure look nice together. We're up eight.

Winnie comes shooting up the floor. He's coming hard and going right for the hoop. I fake like I'm going to take a charge and then scoot to the side and get a piece of the ball as he goes by, and he misses. Tyrone gets the rebound and passes to Al who hits an easy jumper and that's the game. We win by ten.

I'm walking off and Tyrone and Al and Jamal are slapping hands. Robert is wiping his face with a towel. Pruze walks out to meet me. He's wearing a purple team jersey that says RINALDI'S MASONRY. "Look at you. Running ROCK like you own it." He slaps me five.

"Thanks." I'm gulping air. I walk a little with Pruze toward the water fountain. "It's a buster just getting on the court with these guys. I had to argue my way into the game."

"Yeah, that's the way it is, till you show somebody you got a game." He sees Tyrone coming over. "Tyrone, my man! Al! Jumpin' Jamal! What's going on?"

Tyrone says, "We winning ROCK, that's what's going on. Gonna dust your sorry team." But he's smiling and they're all slapping hands.

Pruze says, "See you got my man, Ray. You're lucky. He's a Polack."

Tyrone looks at me with no expression. Al smiles a little. Jamal keeps filling his water bottle from the fountain.

"That's right. My man, Ray. You guys needed a little white power, that's all." Pruze is leaning on Tyrone.

"Oh man, you so full of it. I'll check you out later. You going to Tommy C's?" Tyrone asks.

"Yeah, after we finish here."

"Cool. See ya." The Hayes brothers all go out together.

Pruze slaps me on the back and says, "You got a good team. Al, Jamal, Tyrone. They're tough. Hey, you wanna hang with them a little? Go to Tommy C's party later?"

I'm thinking this is probably not a good idea. I don't really feel like I fit in with all these guys. And I think the party may involve some illegal substances, if I know Pruze.

"Nah. I'll pass this time."

"You don't know what you're missing."

"Maybe I do."

Pruze cracks up. "Maybe you do!"

"Yeah. Hey, thanks, Pruze."

"For what?"

"You know. Putting in a good word for me with Tyrone. I was having some trouble here being the only white boy."

Pruze shakes his head. "Nah. It ain't that way, man. It's 'cause Tyrone didn't know you. If you were purple and had two heads and he knew you could shoot, he'd put you in."

I'm still not sure about that at all, but I don't want to debate it. "Okay, yeah. Have a good one."

We high-five each other. "See you, Ray."

I grab my T-shirt and head for the door, still wearing my red jersey. It's real dark out now. The parking lot is full of guys hanging around.

I pick up my pace, and when I get around the corner, I jog back to Greenville. It's only a ten- or fifteen-minute run, but I'm pretty sweaty when I get there. I walk in and there sitting in my dad's chair eating a plate of pierogies is Walter.

My mom is on the couch next to him. She's wearing her big quilted robe and furry slippers. "Walter came over. I told him to wait for you. That you were going to be done with your game soon."

"Yeah. Thanks, Mom. Hey, Wally."

Walter climbs out of the chair, wiping his mouth with the back of his hand. "What's up, basketball boy?"

"Let's go down to the basement. *Dr. Shock*'ll be on."

"Cool. Thanks, Mrs. W. Those pierogies are dynamite."

Mom smiles. "Anytime. You're always welcome here."

Walter puts the plate in the sink, and we go down and flick on the tube. I grab a towel from the laundry pile and wipe the sweat off.

Walter says, "What's this basketball game?"

I hang the towel on the stair rail. "Nothing much. Playing in a summer league."

"PAL?"

I flop on the couch. "No, a different one."

Walter stretches out and kicks his boots off. "Which?"

"ROCK."

He sits right up. "ROCK? Get out! What are you, underprivileged or something?"

"Shut up. Anybody can do ROCK. It's cool. Me and Pruze are in it."

Walter stares at me, then shakes his head. "Geez. Pretty soon you'll be wantin' government cheese, too."

"Bug off."

Walter has this amazed look on his face. "My old man would freak."

"It's cool."

He rolls his eyes. "If you say so."

I definitely want to change the subject. "You haven't been around much."

"Yeah. I live at the egg stand." He grabs a pillow and puts it behind his head. "Was Malovic at this ROCK thing?"

"Yeah. He runs it. I'm showing him I can play."

"I figured. Mr. Total A-Hole. You know what he told me at the end of school this year? He used all his guidance counselor genius and figured out why my grades suck—I'm lazy. *I'm* lazy! I'd like to see him drag his fat butt around and do the farm in the morning, run the stand, and do school, too."

I turn on the TV. Two boxers are squaring off on each other.

Walter says, "Whoa. Boxing. Leave it on." Then he looks over at me with a big grin, freckles everywhere. "Oh, man. Remember when I taught *you* to box?"

"Oh, yeah. That pea brain Zulik."

We were in fourth grade and this creep named Zulik, this short, red-haired kid who always looked like his butt was itching him or something, was after me every day after school. I'd never had a fight with anybody except wrestling around for fun. Walter saw what was going on. He said, "Ray-Ray, you're going to have to fight him. We got to get you ready."

Yeah, right. What were we going to do? Go to karate school? Then the next day Walter shows up at my house with two pairs of boxing gloves. Real ones. Huge, big, old, cracked brown leather things with dirty, frayed laces. He showed me how to put my left foot forward, hold up my left fist to block and cock my right to throw straight right crosses, and then follow with left jabs. We practiced in my backyard, knocking each other into the grass.

Two weeks later we were playing football over at Teddy Turkowski's house. Teddy and Zulik were pals, always doing crummy stuff together, like stealing little kids' bikes and torturing animals. Made for each other. Zulik was there and he zeroed in on me right away. I tried to ignore him, but after the game he grabbed me by my shirttail as I was leaving and said real loud for everybody, "You're not running away, fairy boy!"

He threw this huge, wild left. I stepped back from it.

"Oh, gonna run, little baby? Run to Mommy." He threw another wild left. I blocked it with my right and hit him two quick, hard left jabs on his nose. He fell backwards onto the grass, scrambled up, and stumbled away crying. That was it. End of problems with Zulik.

Walter laughs. "Hey, I made you what you are today."

I change the channel to *Dr. Shock*. Walter says, "Oooh, check it out. Dr. Shock got a mummy movie."

I turn up the volume. Walter tosses a sock from the laundry basket at me. "You sure this ROCK thing is cool? Nobody's hassling you?"

"What do I look like? A baby?"

"All right. If you need me to give anybody any boxing lessons, just let me know." The mummy appears on the screen and Walter looks totally absorbed. I'm looking at the tube, too, but I'm thinking about basketball. And ROCK. And Walter. And how some things definitely have to stay in their own separate compartments.

chapter six
CHAMPIONSHIP

By the last week of July I'm averaging eight points a game in ROCK. Which is not bad coming off the bench. I'm playing good D, too. Just like in camp. I love shutting people down. Some guys talk trash to me and push and stuff. I just keep this straight face, like I don't even hear it. It makes them crazy and throws their game off even more. I don't know how much of an impression this is making on Malovic, though. When he looks at me I get no expression.

After a couple of games, the rest of the guys start acting real regular with me. Talking and joking and stuff. Especially Al and Tyrone. It's a whole new thing. I was never ever talking to black guys like this before. It's like because of the basketball that we're automatically cool with each other. I mean, Tyrone orders me around and yells a lot, but he does that with everybody. Only Robert and Rudy never say anything to me. On or off the court. Robert doesn't really say much to anybody. Except Rudy.

The way the league ends up, it all comes down to us and

Auto Glass in the final. I show up with Pruze. When we walk in, the place is jammed. People have lawn chairs set up by the doorways. We squeeze our way through. Pruze says, "Big crowd! You'll dig it, Ray-Ray. Light 'em up."

He slaps me on the back and wedges himself into the stands right behind the bench. I walk over to our guys. Al, Jamal, Tyrone, Larry, and Fred are all there standing in a little circle. "Hey, man. Ready to rock?" Al asks with a grin.

"Sure."

Tyrone says, "Okay, good you got here. You almost always late. You on CPT?"

Al and Jamal bust out laughing. I have no idea what he's talking about. "What's CPT?"

Tyrone snaps a towel at me. "Colored People Time, man."

I have to smile. Tyrone looks around. "Don't know where that Robert and Rudy is, either." Just as he says it, Robert and Rudy come bopping in. Rudy is wearing a big leather apple-jack tilted on the side of his head. It must be ninety degrees and he's wearing a leather hat.

"Where you been? Let's warm up," Tyrone says with his lemon-in-the-mouth face.

"Stay cool, jewel. Your man is here," says Rudy, and he pats Robert on the back and massages his shoulders. Rudy acts like Robert's personal assistant or something. It's pretty sickening.

We get on the court and run layups until Malovic blows

the whistle and we huddle up. Tyrone starts talking. "Okay. Al, you and Jamal on the wings. I be center. Robert, you take the point and Rudy, you're back with Robert."

Our guys come out kind of flat. Robert is not playing D on Winnie and Winnie is hot. People in the stands are going, "Oooh, oooh" when he put his jumpers in. The thing with Robert is he can play great defense. He just doesn't do it sometimes.

With Winnie hitting like that and Curly muscling up some inside stuff, we go down ten at the end of the first quarter. At the whistle, Tyrone practically chases Robert back to the bench. "Hey, you little dope! You better play some D!"

Robert tosses a yeah over his shoulder and walks to the water fountain.

I'm looking at Tyrone, trying to catch his eye. I don't want him to forget I'm there. Fred and Larry start getting in Tyrone's face. "When are we playing?"

Tyrone says, "Right now. You go in for Rudy and Robert."

Rudy does his tantrum and sits down. Robert comes back from the water fountain and goes out to the circle for the tap. Larry says, "You sittin', man. I'm on."

Robert says, "BS."

Larry yells to Tyrone, "Hey, Tyrone. Robert ain't sittin'."

Tyrone looks up. "Sit down, Robert. These guys gotta play. Best to be this quarter."

Robert just stands at center court. He's looking at the

floor with his hands on his knees. Malovic says, "Let's go," and he blows the whistle.

Tyrone walks over to Robert, towering over him. "Go sit. You on next quarter again."

Robert keeps staring at the floor like he's alone out there. Tyrone doesn't know what to do. He looks at Malovic. "Coach."

"Yes?"

They walk under the basket talking quietly together. Malovic looks over at Robert. Then he looks back at Tyrone. I figure, all right! Malovic's going to pull Robert's butt right off the floor in front of everybody. Then he whispers something more to Tyrone and I can hear Tyrone say, "But—"

Malovic puts a hand on Tyrone's arm and they walk back out to the center. Tyrone motions to Al. "Al, man. You gotta sit awhile."

Al looks at him, then comes and sits next to me, but we don't say anything. The second quarter starts up and it's the same thing. Robert hits a few from outside and gets some nice drives, but Winnie is killing us because nobody's guarding him. Finally, Jamal comes up to help out on Winnie. As soon as he does, they drop it down low to their open big man. We are down fifteen. We are getting blown out of the championship by a team we already beat by ten! The crowd is hooting at us. Malovic blows the whistle for the half.

Tyrone is like a man on fire. He kicks the bleachers. Robert goes over to get a drink. Malovic puts an arm around his shoulder and is talking real intent in his face. Robert looks at the floor some more.

Larry sits down. He didn't do anything and he knows he's done for tonight. Fred looks a little unsure whether to bother Tyrone right now.

Tyrone says, "Yeah. All right. Ray, Fred, Al, me, and Robert is on."

Rudy is sulking at the end of the bench. Jamal says, "Oh, man. You crazy?"

"What you want me to do?" Tyrone says. Then he whispers, "He won't let me sit Robert. If I don't play these guys, we lose 'cause we break the rules. You know Curly's watching this stuff."

Jamal sits down and stares into space. We go out on the floor for the second half. Winnie comes out hot again, but Robert has shifted off him, now that I'm on the court. It's me and Winnie again. I D up hard, but he gets his first one off and it's good. We're down seventeen.

Tyrone yells as we head up court, "Shut him down!"

Robert takes a wild shot that comes hard off the board and gives them an easy breakaway. We're down nineteen. Tyrone calls time-out. It looks like it's over. We walk off and flop on the bench.

Tyrone says, "We're going full-court press. Ray, you got to shut Winnie down. Now!"

"Yeah."

"I don't want him touching the ball! Right?"

I say, "You got it." I'm not going to let him down.

Tyrone glances back at Malovic hunched over the scorer's table. He wheels around, reaches out, and quick grabs Robert by the face, pulling him up onto his feet with one hand. Robert's eyes bulge. He wiggles out and glares at Tyrone.

Tyrone spits at him, "You listen to me, Little Black Fauntleroy! You better play serious, tight D right now!"

"Yeah, yeah." Robert has this little smart-ass smile on.

Jamal glowers down at him, so does Al. The Hayes brothers form a little box around Robert. Jamal's voice sounds like metal clanking, "Robert, I'm gonna mess you up if you don't."

Robert just smirks, but I can see a change in his eyes. Malovic's not going to be around Jefferson Park when the Hayes brothers pay a visit to Robert's house.

Tyrone gives us our spots and we come out with the press. Curly messes up on the inbounds and throws it right to Tyrone. He jams it home so the rim shakes. The crowd oooohs. "No problem," Curly yells. Then he tries to throw this bomb pass down almost the whole court. I nab it easy, throw it quick to Robert, who dishes to Al going in, and Boom! Jam number two! We're down fifteen.

Our press is getting to them, but Curly won't call time out. They keep trying to get it in and when they do, they're rattled. Robert is playing some D on his man for a change so the press is working. They can't set up and I'm denying

Winnie the ball. They were relying on Winnie for so long, they don't know what to do now.

On offense we're hitting the open man nice and they're tired so they're not picking up on us. At the end of the third quarter we're only down six. We cut thirteen points off their lead in a quarter!

I have my head between my knees. I am so hot. I'm sucking air in and sweating all over the place. We all look like we've been swimming. Malovic has these little kids drying the court with towels at every whistle.

We win the tap for last quarter. Tyrone brings it up and passes to me. They're confused about who's playing who and I'm open so I move to the top of the key and fire it up. Boom! It's in. We're down four. Tyrone calls out, "Way to hit it, Ray."

Finally Auto Glass gets it together. They set some nice picks for Winnie and he gets open enough to buss it home or drop it inside and we go down eight again. Then Robert gets hot. We go up three times in a row and he hits his J all three times and suddenly we're down by two. They call time-out. I look at the clock for the first time in ages. One minute to go! Tyrone huddles us up. "Okay. Now we press their butts off! We press their juice out! Feed Robert. He's hot."

One thing about Tyrone—he doesn't hold a grudge. He just wants to win. Robert stares at the floor. Rudy is patting him on the back.

We get on again and Winnie brings it up. I can see he's

looking in, but then he fakes me and heads for the hoop on the drive. He puts it up, but he's off balance and Tyrone slaps it back. It's heading out-of-bounds right near me. I run for it, but it's skipping along fast so I dive, get a hand on it, and tap it back toward the court. My body smacks the floor and I skid a couple of feet on my chest and side.

Al scoops up the loose ball and hits Jamal going down court. Jamal lays it up and in. Tie game. Thirty seconds on the clock. Curly calls time-out. Al helps me up, slaps me five, and says, "Nice save, man."

Even Jamal gives me a nod. Tyrone's got his arms around Jamal and Al. He gulps out the words. "Okay. Press 'em. There's a whole thirty seconds. They got to shoot. They gonna go inside to Curly. Or maybe they look to Winnie. No fouls. If we get the ball, call time."

We go out and they inbound up the sideline and set up. Twenty seconds. Winnie gets it off their wing. He tries to move around me, but Al comes over to help. Winnie backs out, and fakes to the wing and bounces a pass into Curly. Curly tries to power over Tyrone. Tyrone stays straight up, making sure Malovic can see it's no foul. Curly's shot goes off the back iron, and Jamal grabs the rebound. He calls time.

Twelve seconds on the clock. My lungs are burning. It hurts to breathe deep. I can only do these little shallow breaths and I'm dizzy. My chest is stinging, too. It's got a nice wood burn on it.

Tyrone is huffing and gasping the words out, "This is it.

Al, inbound to Jamal or Robert. Ray, stay out of there, I don't want you handling the ball. Get on the opposite wing. Look for me inside. Jamal, if you get it, go to the hoop. We get the close shot or the foul. Let's go. We gonna win this right now."

We set up. Al is really under pressure on the inbounds, but he gets it to Robert. Robert speeds around Winnie heading for the hoop, but they come off Tyrone and jam Robert up. Five seconds. Robert can't see over them to get it to Tyrone.

Robert passes back to Jamal. He's covered. Three seconds. I'm wondering, is he going to try to force it. Then he whips it to me crosscourt without even looking. Everybody's surprised. Including me!

Two seconds on the clock and I'm holding the ball and I'm open. My man fell back on Tyrone. Tyrone said not to shoot from the outside, but I know I don't have a good enough drive to head for the hoop and he's double-teamed.

One second.

I got no time to do anything but shoot.

I go straight up. My man starts toward me, but he's too late. I flick my wrist and let the ball fly smooth off my fingers. It's in the air and I hear the buzzer. If it goes, it's good. I watch it arc toward the hoop on my way down.

Piff!

The net does its little kick.

The guys are all over me. Tyrone, Jamal, Al, Larry, Fred. I can't believe it! It's like one of my driveway dreams. The place is yelling and screaming. After we all jump around for a while we finally line up to shake hands with the other team. Winnie comes along. He bumps me five and says, "Nice buss there, man."

"Thanks. Nice game yourself." It was big of him to say that after the hassling I did on him on D. You can tell a lot about somebody by the way they are on the court. You can tell Winnie is all right. He kept his cool.

I come off and Pruze gives me a hug. "Hey, superstar!"

Tyrone high fives Pruze, "Told you he was a player, Pruze. Told you all along."

Pruze puts his hands on his hips, "Oh yeah, right! You were his number one fan, that's why you wouldn't even give him a shirt when he showed up."

Tyrone looks off to the side. "Don't know what you're talkin' about. You doin' too many of them psychedelic drugs." Tyrone winks at me and puts out his hand for me to slap him five. In a low voice he says, "Way to hit, man. Way to be clutch."

Robert and Rudy walk by on their way out. Malovic is there by the door. He slaps Robert five and Rudy too. He pats Robert on the back.

"Look at that," I say to Pruze. "Robert wouldn't leave the court tonight when Tyrone told him to and now Malovic is congratulating him."

"Don't worry about it. He's got this thing with Robert and a couple of these other guys."

"Like what?"

"Like he feels sorry for them. If they're real goof-ups like Robert, he takes 'em under his wing or something. Plus, if they've been playing for him for a while, they're real tight. Robert is both."

I take a big drink of water. It tastes like the best drink in the world. "That stinks."

"Yeah. Malovic thinks he's doing a good deed, but they're just playing him for a fool."

Me and Pruze head to the door. I've never felt this up before. I can't stop grinning.

We get to the door and Malovic is still there. I figure he's going to say something to me about winning the game and all, but when we get there, he looks the other way and starts calling to some kid in the crowd like he had something he had to say to him right away. Pruze and I walk on by and out the door. I mumble "Jerk-off" under my breath. Pruze chuckles.

Shoot. I don't care. But in the back of my head I gotta wonder if he can ignore me now, when I just won a championship right in front of him.

chapter seven
INVITATION TO GREENVILLE

I am high all that week after the championship. I even feel good pulling weeds out in the ninety-degree heat. Saturday, right after dinner, there's a knock on the porch door. I peer through the screen. It's Walter. "Walter. Too late, man. Kielbasa's all gone."

He ignores this. "Ray-Ray, I need a major favor."

I unlatch the screen door. "This is sounding very scary."

He stays right there on the porch. That's when I notice he's *dressed*. With clean pants and a striped golf shirt. He even has dress shoes on. I didn't know Walter *owned* dress shoes.

"Listen. I'm going bowling with Stella Gorski in about an hour and—"

"You got a date with Stella?" Stella's all right. Long blond hair. Lot of makeup, a little hard-edged, but good-looking. She goes to the Catholic high school, OLC.

"Yeah, man. And I need somebody to cover the stand. It's only from seven till nine."

I tighten the screws a little. "I don't know. I was gonna watch *Animal Planet*."

Walter whacks me in the shoulder. "C'mon, man! This is serious."

"I'll say. Stella should get some therapy if she's thinking about going out with you."

Walter hits me again. "I'm serious."

I lean against the door frame. Me, Stella, and Walter went to elementary school together, made confirmation and first communion together, been to church youth group parties together, but I never thought she would date Walter. Geez. It's hard to picture anyone dating Walter.

Walter begins pleading. His eyebrows go up on his forehead. "C'mon, man. Help me out here." He has his hands together like he's praying.

"All right. All right. I'll do it as big favor to you, you punk."

Walter jumps in the air pumping his fist. "Yessss!"

"So what do I do?"

Walter gives me a key for opening up the case. He drives me there, shows me everything like in five seconds, then speeds out of the parking lot honking his horn. Fortunately, there's only five customers all night. I walk home and chill out. While I'm watching TV the phone rings at about eleven. Walter yells over the other end, "I am the man!"

"How was it?"

"I am in love!"

"You mean, you're in lust."

"Whatever. I got me a woman. Thank you. Thank you. Thank you!"

I laugh. But it makes me think about how I've got to be more proactive on the girl scene. I'm not bad-looking. People don't run away screaming, but dancing with your neighbors at church socials is not the same as going out with somebody. I don't want to go out with anyone just to say I'm going out with someone, either. I'd like to go out with Jennifer Lopez. Or Stacey Steck. But that's not going to happen anytime soon.

After ROCK is over, I just keep playing ball with Pruze all through August. Pruze and I don't socialize much past that. He's into a pretty hardy party scene, which is not me. I also do my usual routine every day on my court in the driveway. Now that school's starting up again, I have to get up earlier to do it. I'm sweating by the time I start walking to school. Some people would think that's a big deal. Hard practice. To me, it's fun. I could shoot forever like that.

First day back Walter and I meet at our usual table. The school smells new like it always does in September. Polish, wax, disinfectant. I look at my schedule card: AP Biology, English IV Honors, Calculus, U.S. History Honors, lunch, gym, Spanish III. The best class is going to be history with Mr. Paterson. I'm looking forward to it. Paterson is great.

"Welcome back to the cell block, my man. What do ya

got first period?" Walter asks. He's got nothing with him—no notebooks, no binder, no backpack.

"AP Biology."

He snickers. "Another egghead class." He's wearing a tank top and shorts. He's got a farmer tan and his arms are looking huge

"What do you have then, macho man?"

The bell rings and we get up.

Walter puts one hand on his hip and traces something in the air with his other hand. "I have Ahhhht. So I can express myself."

We walk to the corner and head in different directions.

"Don't eat the paint, Picasso."

He makes a dopey face. "Yeah. I'll see you at lunch."

When I come into Paterson's history class later that morning, there sitting in the front row is Winnie, the little guard from Auto Glass. He's never been in any of my classes before. On the way to my seat he nods at me and I nod back. I sit two seats behind him. Nobody's at the desk between us.

He turns completely around and faces me. "Hey, man. How you doin'?" He stretches across the desk with his fist out for a bump. "Winnie."

I'm a little surprised. I didn't expect to see him in honors history. Then right away I feel stupid that I'm surprised that Winnie is smart, but my hand goes out like a reflex for the bump. "Yeah. I remember." Maybe I'm the only guy he knows in here. "How you doin'? I'm Ray."

"Doin' okay, 'cept for school startin' up and cramping my style." He's dressed real sharp with these cool baggy pants, boots, and a white knit shirt.

He's looking right at me. I figure I should talk. "You ever have Paterson before?"

"Yeah. Last year for Government. He's good."

"Yeah."

Then Mr. Paterson starts in with, "How many of you know why America came into existence?" Typical Paterson question. He rarely asks anything like names or dates. He's always asking how or why.

After class Winnie and I walk out the door right next to each other. "Can't believe you beat us in ROCK, man," he says, shaking his head.

I shrug. "Well, we had a lot of power with the Hayes brothers."

"Yeah, you had everybody but their dad."

I turn right and Winnie does too. He asks, "Where you goin'?"

"Lunch."

"Yeah, me too."

We don't say anything else until we get to the door to the cafeteria. We both hesitate. "Later, man," he says.

"Yeah, later."

Then we head off in different directions.

I see Stoshy and Gerard in line, so I put my lunch down

at our regular table and go over and get behind them. We get our drinks. I always get orangeade. That's about all I ever buy in the cafeteria. That and ice cream sandwiches. The actual cooked food is terrible. We walk back to our table and have to pass right alongside a table where Winnie is sitting with Al Hayes. "Hey, Ray. Man, what's goin' on?" Al says.

He reaches out for a bump. I bump him while Stoshy stands by and gives them a nod. Gerard copies Stoshy, then they both start walking to our table. There's an empty seat next to Winnie and two next to Al. It would be the most natural thing in the world to just sit right down there and keep on talking.

I say, "Later, guys," and follow Stoshy and Gerard to *our* lunch table.

When I go into history the next day, Paterson is chalking stuff up on the board. He's kind of a small guy with dark hair. A little on the chubby side, but with this real glint in his eye and a little half smile. He always looks like he knows something you don't. Which is true ninety-nine percent of the time.

Winnie is writing in his notebook, his pen skipping along the paper. As I walk by he glances up at me. Real friendly he says, "What's up?"

"Nothing. What's that?" I say nodding toward his notebook.

"Tryin' to finish the homework. First day and he gives us

homework."

Even though we played real hard against each other in ROCK, here he is being friendly and cool. I'm surprised how we're talking. We even walk out together into the hall after class again. "You playing any ball?" Winnie asks me.

"Yeah. A lot of one-on-one with Pruze in my driveway."

"You got a hoop in your driveway?

"Yep."

Winnie nods. "That's nice." He shakes his head. "Heh. I bet me and Al could wipe you and Pruze's butts all over your rinky-dink driveway." He's smiling.

I shake my head. "No way."

"We'd use you up. I'm tellin' you." He puffs out his chest goofin' around and bumps into me.

I wave a hand at him and keep walking. "Get out."

He stops, puts his hands out, palms up. "Anytime, man. You name it."

I stop.

He's smiling big-time. "Well? Can you handle it?"

It would be fun playing those two with Pruze. "How about Saturday?"

Winnie smiles big. "All right then. Give me some directions."

"Where?"

He crinkles up his forehead. "To your house. That's where your driveway is, right?"

Oh, man! I forgot we had started by talking about my

driveway. I just invited a black guy to my house! Two black guys! "Uh, yeah."

Winnie studies me for a fraction of a second. I can tell he picked up on me hesitating. Then he says, "Cool. Like one o'clock, okay? I got stuff I got to do in the morning. And tell Pruze he has to wear deodorant."

We both laugh and the tension melts away. "All right. I'll tell him."

Winnie tears a piece of paper out of his notebook. "Write me down some directions, man." I do and we walk over to the cafeteria, stop for a second, and then split at the entrance again. I head over to our table. Walter, Stoshy, and Gerard are already there. I don't bother to tell them.

After school I tell my dad, though. I say these guys are coming over to play ball on Saturday. Then I tell him their names and where they're from. I do everything but actually say, "Dad, black guys are coming to the house," but I know he gets the message. He is unfazed. I leave it to him to inform Mom.

Mom eventually talks about it in a roundabout way while we're watching TV that night. "So your father said you have some friends coming over Saturday."

"Yeah. To play basketball."

She's looking at the TV but talking to me. "That's nice that you're making new friends."

"Yep." I notice she's twisting her wedding ring around and around.

"When I was little, Franklin was very different. Bridgeton, too. On Sundays everybody used to walk to church dressed up and stay dressed up all day. Then we would eat with all the family at someone's house. Every Sunday. We would take turns."

I nod. "I remember you saying."

"You don't see that anymore. So many people have moved away." She sighs. "And new people move in. Like your new friends." The wedding ring is going round and round and round.

"Yeah. They're nice guys."

She smiles and nods. "I'm sure they are." It's like she's reassuring herself. She is definitely nervous.

To be honest, I am, too. I keep telling myself, it's no big deal. They're just guys I know. I'm not trying to prove anything, but I feel like people might think I am. Maybe I should call Winnie and tell him I got sick or my driveway's messed up. But then, what am I scared about? What's anybody going to say? I decide, just suck it up. It'll be cool.

I'm waiting in the driveway after lunch with Pruze on Saturday. At about one thirty I see the two of them come crossing Montgomery Avenue, bouncing a ball.

I call over, "Hey, you're late. Little scared?"

Winnie yells, "Scared Pruze might fart. That's all I'm scared about. Last time he laid one in the locker room and we all liked to die."

Pruze laughs. "Just wait, Skinny Winnie."

We play three games to twenty-one. They win the first and we win the second. In the last game me and Winnie get our hands on the ball at the same time and we're pulling. In a real game it would have been a jump ball, but when you play outside, street ball, you just keep pulling till somebody comes away with it.

Winnie tucks it back under his arm, but I hang on and we both go down on the blacktop. The ball squirts out and we go scrambling after it.

"Get back, you animal!" he yells.

I grab his sweatshirt and pull it and toss him aside off the court and into the grass. Pruze grabs the ball and goes for the hoop with Al chasing him. Winnie gets back up and jumps on my back and we start wrestling. We're both laughing so hard we can't really wrestle. I finally stuff grass down his neck and he backs off.

"You one nutty boy, Ray."

"Look who's talking."

Pruze coming running over, his arms pumping in the air. "We won. I just scored the last bucket."

Al yells, "Oh, man! You did shit. You walked!"

We flop in the grass. I run the garden hose over and we take turns guzzling the cold water. I'm grinning with relief. We did it. We played. We hung out. It was cool. Pruze says, "Hey, Ray. I heard Stacey was looking for you."

Winnie and Al wolf howl together. *Everybody* knows Stacey. I saw her twice during the summer catching some rays in a bikini near the lake and it was nearly cardiac arrest.

"Yeah, but I been too busy. She'll have to take a number."

Pruze says, "Who you been busy with? Yourself?"

Al and Winnie hoot while I give Pruze a good rap in the arm.

Winnie says, "Hey let's play again over the school courts Monday."

I spin the ball on my finger. "I'm good."

Pruze says, "Okay."

Al says, "Yeah. We got to practice. We're gonna be the nuuucleus of this team this year!"

Winnie laughs. "Damn, Al. You been readin' your biology."

"Damn straight. Biology, astrology, all those -ologies."

Then I hear a truck engine—loud and clanky. My neck stiffens. I turn my whole body and point it at Pruze and look right at him.

The engine is getting closer. I keep my face focused on Pruze like I'm listening real intently. The truck drives slowly by. I see it out of the corner of my eye, but I keep my head turned and my gaze locked on Pruze. He looks back at me. I can tell he knows.

The truck cruises on down the street and turns. I won't look up till it's totally gone. I don't want Walter to know that I saw him.

chapter eight
COACH T

We come in from church on Sunday morning and the phone is ringing. I grab it. "Hello?"

"Hey, dude. What's up?" It's Walter.

"I'm just gettin' back from mass."

There's quiet for a second. "Hey. Listen. I got to see you. How about we meet at the lake in an hour?"

Oh, man. I know he's going to want to get into Al and Winnie being at my house. This is not a conversation I want to have.

"Yeah. Okay."

"See you then."

I change my clothes and shoot some hoops. Then make my way over. Walter's truck is already there. He's sitting on the hood throwing stones at the geese. They strut away, taking their time, like no big deal.

"Wally Gator!"

"Ray-Ray!"

I walk up. My heart is beating fast. How to start? Walter,

it's none of your business. Walter, these guys are guys from the team. Walter—"

"How's it going?"

"Okay. What's up?"

"You're a big-time tutor, right?" He hops off the hood and ducks into the driver's side window.

"Yeah. Kind of like Einstein."

He pulls out a book and shoves it at me. "I'm trying to do this stuff."

I recognize the cover. It's Algebra I. This is the book I had in eighth grade.

Walter looks at the lake. "Usually I don't give a shit, but this new teacher, Mrs. Harper, is busting my butt. Even was calling my house, saying if I just applied myself I could do good and all that bull. My old man does *not* want the school calling the house. So I was thinking maybe you could help me get through this and get this lady off my back."

I am incredibly relieved. "Yeah. No problem. I love algebra."

Walter smiles. "You're really sick. You know that?"

"All right. What chapter are you doing?"

We spread the stuff out on one of the picnic tables and work for an hour. By the end he can do all the chapter review exercises and he got them all right but two.

"Geez. You're like a prodigy, man. You'll be doing nuclear physics next."

Walter messes up my hair. "Thanks. You the man, Ray."

"Yeah. How's things with Stella?"

Walter tosses his book in the truck. "Total groove thang."

"When are you going to set me up with one of her friends?"

"Anytime. Linda Latawiec is always hanging with her."

"No! Not Linda." Linda has a pierced eyebrow and a spider tattoo on her neck.

"Man. You're too picky. Linda has everything you need, two—"

"Forget I asked."

Walter never says a thing about that Saturday. We do algebra every couple of weeks, whenever he's got a chapter test coming up. Usually in the morning in the cafeteria before school. I'm enjoying it. It makes me think more than ever that being a teacher is the thing for me. I just might be pretty good at it.

The other new thing going on is that once a week or so, me, Winnie, Al, and Pruze play some ball together down at the school courts. We're tuning up for tryouts. It's a good two-on-two matchup. It's not something I'm exactly hiding from Walter, but I don't bother to mention it, either. Compartments. That's how I've got it organized.

I am a senior. I am seventeen years old. And I have never actually *made* a basketball team. I have to *make* varsity. You can't play JV as a senior. That's what I'm thinking as I walk into the locker room for the first day of tryouts. Malovic, here I come.

I dress slow and careful, like wearing my stuff the right way is going to help. I've got on my lucky red laces. I know it's stupid, but I've got to wear 'em. I decided they were lucky since I wore them that first game in ROCK. I got new sneakers, but I wear the same laces. It's like a ritual or something.

Out in the gym, there's the usual tryout mob and the balls everywhere. It's funny, it doesn't bother me anymore that there's only a handful of us who are white. I grab a rebound and take it to the top of the key. Rudy's standing there with his hair all high and stupid and greasy on his head. He sees me coming and sneers. "You here again?"

I take a step back and put both my hands in front of my face. "Back away, man. Your hair's scaring me."

Rudy tilts his head back trying to look bad. "You wanna—"

"Hey, check it out." It's Al nodding his head toward the gym office. Things get very quiet except for the bouncing balls.

Waltzing out of the locker room wearing his same high black Nikes and gray sweats is Malovic, but next to him is this tall guy with a gray golf shirt and dark blue shorts. High white socks and high white sneakers. The shorts have creases like they were ironed. The guy is black.

Rudy forgets about me and stares along with everyone else. Al pulls up his socks and tightens his laces. I do the same even though I've already done it in the locker room.

Ziggy comes over and nods toward the black guy. "Who's he?"

"I have no idea."

The black guy stands by the locker room talking to Mr. Paley, the old freshman coach.

A whistle slices the din of balls bouncing. "Balls away. Have a seat at half-court." Malovic calls it out.

Malovic and the guy walk out together with Paley trailing. Pruze slides in next to me. Powell is the only one who keeps moving, running around picking up the balls, putting them on the racks. Malovic waits until we're all seated. "Good afternoon, boys. I'd like to begin with an important announcement about our program."

He clears his throat. "I'd like to inform you at this time that I will be assuming the duties of the newly created position of athletic director here at Franklin High School. I wanted you all to hear it first from me. I will no longer officially be coaching."

The place is completely silent except for breathing. I look at Pruze. He's staring back at me, bugging his eyes out.

"After a comprehensive search we were fortunate enough to find Mr. Fenton Thomas to assume leadership of our varsity basketball program. I know you will give him your full support, cooperation, and best efforts."

He starts clapping and we all follow along.

Rudy says in this little falsetto voice, "Fennnnton." Robert giggles and shakes his head.

Malovic ignores them and goes on. "Many of you proba-bly already know Mr. Paley. He will also assume the newly created position of junior varsity coach." He claps and we all join in again.

Malovic—is—not—coaching! I feel a smile tug at my mouth.

The applause dies down and then he says, "I want you all to know that I will still be very much a part of your team this year as well."

Then I swear he looks right at me and says, "I will be assisting Mr. Thomas and Mr. Paley in transitioning this team to new leadership."

What does that mean? "Transitioning"?

"As athletic director I am still available to you and will continue to support the program one hundred percent. But now let me turn this tryout over to Mr. Thomas."

Mr. Thomas nods at Malovic who takes a few steps back grinning. "Thank you, Mr. Malovic."

He has a big neck and short dark hair with a little gray at the temples.

"Gentleman. Welcome to Franklin High's varsity basket-ball tryouts. I'm Coach Thomas. It is a pleasure and an honor to be here." He sounds like James Earl Jones. He pronounces everything real carefully.

"I appreciate you being here today, too, and your willing-ness to try out for this team. There are forty-two of you. Unfortunately, that's about sixteen too many for our squads."

Rudy yells, "You right. We got to get rid of some of these lamos."

Robert stares into space like he's lost. Malovic shakes his head with a little grin. He thinks that stuff is cute. Coach Thomas says, "What's your name, son?"

Rudy is grinning, all proud that he's getting a personal introduction to the coach. "Rudy."

"Rudy what?"

"Rudy Robinson."

"Give me five, Rudy Robinson."

Rudy gets up. He's got an even bigger grin on his face. He holds his hand up. "High five me then, brother."

Guys are laughing under their breath.

"Five laps."

Rudy's face goes slack. He drops his hands. "For what? I was agreein' wit' you."

Coach Thomas doesn't move anything but his lips. "Give me five laps, now, and please do not interrupt me again."

Rudy pimp rolls over to the sideline, mumbling under his breath. Coach Thomas responds, "Too slow. Too much talking. Make it seven laps."

Rudy looks up and sees Coach Thomas standing there like a big tree. He looks over at Malovic who is shifting his weight from foot to foot and studying his shiny black Nikes. Rudy starts his laps.

"Just a word to the wise, gentlemen. No nonsense. We don't have time for it." He calls over to Rudy, "Faster, Robinson."

Rudy shuffles along a little faster.

"We will keep twelve players on varsity and twelve on junior varsity. There will be two designated swingmen who can play on either squad, so we are looking at twenty-six players in total." Coach looks from face to face. "This means there are going to be many good players who will have to be let go."

Pruze elbows me and whispers with a straight face, "Like you, man." I don't elbow back. I don't want to do a thing that could hurt my chances in any possible way.

Coach Thomas takes a few steps and stops. "I also need you to know, that what you have done in the past for other teams may be commendable, but does not apply to making *this* team. If you want a spot, you will have to earn it. Understood?"

There's lots of mumbling. "Yeah, uh-huh."

Rudy flops down with the group again. I know he didn't do seven laps already.

"All right, let's get warmed up. Coach Paley, would you please start our group on calisthenics? And Mr. Robinson . . ."

Rudy is breathing all hard but he manages a "Yeah, Coach?"

"Please get up and finish your laps. You have two more to go."

Paley starts us up and for the next fifteen minutes all we do is jumping jacks, push-ups, sit-ups, and stretches. We're all huffing and sweating, but this stuff doesn't bother me. In fact it gets the chill off and gets me revved up. Coach Thomas sits at a scorer's table that's set up on the sideline at half-court. "Say 'Present' when we call your name."

Malovic sits down next to him at the table. I wish he would get the hell out of here. Coach Thomas starts calling out our names and we keep doing jumping jacks till he gets through all forty-two guys.

"Good. Take a seat down on the half line and count off by twos."

Everybody's out of breath, but we croak out the numbers.

"Ones on this basket. Twos on the other. I want you to start shooting jumpers from outside the key. Follow your shot. Get the rebound. Pass it back and get to the end of the line."

We line up and run the drill. Rudy is behind me. "Don't need to follow my shot. Goes right in," he says to the air.

"Yeah, you're like Superman or something."

"Shut up, Ray. You ain't gonna make this team. You should go home now. Save yourself some trouble."

I don't look at him. "You ran some nice laps, Rudy. You should go out for track."

Rudy snarls, "Keep messing with me, Ray. See what happens."

"Hey, Ray!" It's Al yelling as he passes the ball back to me. I look up just in time, take the pass, move down on the right wing. Pull up. Let it go. Swish. Yes!

I scoop up the rebound and fire a pass as hard as I can at Rudy's head with a big smile.

I hit every one of my jumpers in the drill, but I'm not sure if Coach Thomas saw. That's a tough thing about try-outs. Sometimes you do some great stuff and nobody sees it.

We do all the usual tryout drills: dribbling, rebounding, weave, passing, layups. I'm good on everything, really, but the dribbling. I do okay in the scrimmages, too. Hit two nice jumpers.

At the end we do our line-back sprints. The whistle blows and we go. I'm pounding the wood. I can see Robert working hard to stay right with me. Robert had a great try-out. He was really hot and hit just about everything he threw up. I stare at him as we go and he stares back. It's like a little personal contest.

Finally we all stop, breathing hard, sucking air. Robert and I finished first together.

Coach Thomas says real calm, "Thank you, gentleman. For those who are still interested, we will continue tomorrow at three fifteen sharp and finish at four thirty." He walks off with Paley and Malovic to the coach's office. He walks straight up like a rod's down the middle of his back.

Winnie jogs by and slaps me on the back. "Lookin' good, man."

"Thanks, man."

Malovic is jabbering away in Coach Thomas's ear, an arm around his back. I swear he looks back at me again, like he's telling me, "I'm not gone yet."

chapter nine
LAST CHANCE

The next morning I find Walter stretched out in the cafeteria between two chairs. I walk in and pull one of the chairs just a little. He jumps up. "Man!"

"Wake up, sleeping beauty."

"Geez. You almost killed me." He wipes the sleep from his eyes, sits up, and sips his Coke. "How's your b-ball thing yesterday?"

"It's okay." I sit down. "Could be good. We got a new coach."

"That's what I hear." Walter studies me a second. "Heard he's a bruh-thah."

"Yep."

"Figures."

"He's not Malovic. That's a real plus for me."

Walter laughs. "Yeah. If you say so. Still not too late for wrestling."

"Nah, I'll leave that to you and Stella."

Walter grins and starts singing "My Girl." I hold my ears.

Then from across the cafeteria comes Stacey Steck making a beeline for us. I sit up. I quick press my cowlick down. She comes right over, pulls up a chair, and puts a clipboard on the table in front of us. My heart is jumping out of my chest, and I am sweating. All in five seconds.

"Hi, guys!" She's all smiles.

I smile too. "Hi, Stacey."

"How's it going?"

I say, "Good."

Walter says, "It just got a lot better."

Stacey shakes her head like it's not worth responding. "I wanted to see if you would sign my petition."

Walter leans back. "Sign something? I don't know." He's leering. "What's in it for me?"

Stacey shrugs. "Well, let's see. I don't tell Mr. Gallo that you skipped last period on Friday and went to Lutch's Bar with Teddy."

Walter's eyes pop. "How do you—"

She laughs. "My cousin tends bar there. Anyway, I want to start up a new club here at school, and I need to get a hundred signatures to show there's enough student support."

I want to demonstrate to Stacey that I still have the capacity for speech. "What's the club?"

She locks those green eyes on me. "Multicultural Awareness Club. To promote understanding, awareness, and friendship among the various cultures represented in our school and community."

Walter grabs the pen. "Don't tell Gallo. I'll sign anything you want. Multi-Alien Club, whatever."

She laughs, watches Walter, then passes me the pen and paper when he's done. While I sign it I try to think of something clever to say. Something fun, light, and friendly.

Nothing comes.

Stacey scoops up the papers. "Thanks, guys. Knew I could count on the neighborhood boys." Then she scoots off with a wave.

Walter shakes his head. "Man, she is something."

"Yeah."

The bell rings and we hop up. We go out the door and split. "Later, Ray-Ray."

"Later, Big W."

I walk upstairs to history. I think about Stacey. What a totally cool girl. It's hard to believe she's from Greenville. Walking into history I see Winnie in his seat.

"Ray, what's goin' on?"

"Hey."

"Ready for tryouts today?"

I slide into my seat. "Ready as I'm going to be."

Winnie has a toothpick in his mouth. He works it to the side. "I'll see you in there. You, me, and Coach T."

Cute rhyme. Coach T. First time I've heard anybody call him that. Then Mr. Paterson is talking and we immediately start taking notes.

At three thirty we're all back on the half-court line just like yesterday. This is my last-last-last chance of all time to make it. My last high school tryout. Coach Thomas is there wearing blue shorts and a white golf shirt this time.

"Gentleman. This will be our final day of tryouts. We are down to thirty-five players, which allows everyone a little more opportunity. I will post the list of team members tomorrow morning at eight in the boys' locker room. Practice will begin the following day at three thirty. Any questions?"

Rudy raises his hand. He's operating with a little more respect after the laps yesterday. "Yeah, Coach. What about our shoe sizes?"

Coach T stands there looking at Rudy. "What about your shoe sizes?"

"Well, you know, like usually at the end of tryouts, the manager comes around and asks our shoe size, if you made the team, to provide you with your shoes."

"That's not a procedure I'll be using."

Rudy slips back to his usual stupid self. "Why not?"

Coach T walks over to Rudy. "Well, Mr. Robinson. I have to think about what I'm going to see today. I have to think about what kind of team we can put together. I'm going to think about it tonight. We have plenty of time to get shoe sizes."

Rudy opens up his mouth again. "Where's Mr. Malovic at then?"

T pauses. "Mr. Malovic has other duties to attend to."

Rudy still goes on. "He said he would be transitioning us and stuff."

T looks at Rudy directly again. "Mr. Malovic gave us a good deal of his time yesterday. The rest of the process will be handled by Mr. Paley and myself."

Then there's this little mumbly, froggy voice. "He tole us he was goin' be here." It's Robert! Robert never says much about anything. He's looking at the ground, with his head all loose like he's too cool to care, but he thought he'd ask anyway.

Rudy chimes in, "Yeah. He tole me and Robert."

T stays steady. "That was Mr. Malovic's original intention, but we've made some changes." He claps his hands. "So, let's get started."

Rudy looks at Robert with his mouth open. Robert just looks up at T. It sounds to me like Malovic got told to stay home. This is T's team. How excellent is this!

We start doing cali's and running sprints. I'm feeling real good with no Malovic around. I do good in the drills. Good defense. Actually, real good defense. Hit some jumpers. Miss only two. Finally with about twenty minutes left we get to the scrimmaging. Coach Paley splits us into seven teams of five. Each team gets to run on the court for five minutes against another team. That's all the time you get.

My team is me, Winnie, Ziggy, this little guy from ROCK called D-Man, and Pruze. We're on the sidelines, waiting to be called. Winnie starts goofing. "Look at this," he says. "How I'm supposed to win? I get saddled with three white boys and a pygmy."

D-Man who's like five feet five, says, "Who's a pygymy?"

Pruze laughs, "Aw, Winnie, man. You're lucky you got some brains on your team for a change."

Winnie swivels his head all around. "Where's that at? I got three Polish boys and D-Man. Now that's a real brain trust!"

"Team Six, up! Team Seven, up!" calls Coach Thomas.

We're the last two teams to run. Everybody else is sitting on the sidelines watching us. D-Man says, "Ooh. Seven Up. We're a soda."

Winnie says, "Oh D, be quiet. Let's go. Remember, give me the ball. None of you has any kind of shot."

D-Man inbounds to Winnie mumbling, "Yeah, yeah. You're so cool."

Ziggy and I are at the forwards and Pruze is center. We run pretty good. I get in a couple of nice passes and rebounds, but no shots. Meanwhile, Robert is on the other team and he sinks three jumpers in a row.

They miss one from the corner. Pruze pulls down the rebound and fires it to Winnie. Winnie dribbles hard up the middle. I stay out on the wing. Winnie hits the foul line. He looks left. I come up to the high post and set the pick. Winnie runs his man right into me. I roll off and down into the corner. My man and Winnie's stay with him. Winnie dishes it to me and there I am, wide open in one of my favorite spots, the right corner.

I go straight up. Release off the fingers at the top. It's got a nice arc. It looks good.

Clang! It hits the back rim and bounces off. Pruze grabs the rebound and stuffs it down the hole. I glance back to the sidelines and Coach Thomas is looking right at me. Paley blows the whistle. Coach writes on his clipboard then calls out, "Okay, enough for today. Line up for sprints."

Damn! Double damn! The one time today he's looking for sure, I miss an open shot. And right near the end of the practice, so he'll remember it.

Then it's over. Like that. At the end Coach T thanks everybody and makes us clap for ourselves for putting in a good effort. I notice Robert not clapping.

Me and Pruze walk out together. Paley and T sit down with the clipboard between them at the scorer's table. I would love to see that clipboard.

Pruze pokes me. "Don't stare like it's the zoo, man."

I poke him back, and we all go into the locker room. Pruze's locker is next to mine. I sit on the bench and look at my shoes. I can't believe I'm going to blow my chance with this new coach.

Pruze opens his locker. "What's wrong with you, man?"

"Nothing."

He takes out his towel and puts it around his neck. "It's that shot you took at the end, right?"

"I don't know. Yeah."

"Hey. You set the pick, you rolled, you went to the open spot, you took the shot. Who shoots a hundred percent?"

"I don't know."

"Quit moping then." He snaps me with his towel. "Where's your Polish pride?" Then he yells so everyone in the locker room can hear, "Remember, we're *Polacks* here!"

Winnie calls over from the next row, "Maybe you a bunch of sorry Polacks over there, but we not over here."

"Damn straight," someone else from Winnie's row yells.

"Well, yeah, you're right." Pruze stops on the way to the shower. "We can't all be so lucky."

There's some more yelling back and forth. I don't shower. I just get my clothes on. I don't want to hang around and discuss my shot. Nothing to do now but go home and wait for tomorrow—and the list.

chapter ten
THE LIST

The red numbers on the night table clock let me know—4:15
a.m. Last time I looked it was 4:09 a.m. Time before that,
4:01 a.m.

I roll over and double my pillow under my head. The list
is going to be up. I tell myself, go back to sleep. There's nothing you can do about it now. But the little self-talk is not real
effective.

I say a prayer instead, "God, please let me make the team.
Please put my name on that list." I feel stupid praying for
things like that. Do I pray about my Aunt Joan's cancer?
Starving kids in Africa? No. I pray about making a basketball
team.

At six the alarm finally beeps. Not like there's a big need.

I shower, get dressed, eat, grab the books, and hustle to
school. I go in the side door near the gym. Now that I'm
here after all that rushing around, I just stand in the hall. It's
7:55. First bell is at 8:10. I still have time. I walk past the
locker-room door. If I don't actually see the list there's still a

chance I'm on it, even if I'm really not. It's a stupid little game, but I guess I'm playing it for as long as I can.

I walk right by the cafeteria. I don't need to hear Walter's comments. He hasn't been bugging me about going out, which is a nice surprise. I guess he figures it's a given. Even so, I want to be on my own right now.

I stop by the courtyard and look in through the glass. It's bright sunshine and Teddy Turkowski is in there already in his big blue peacoat, catching a smoke in the cold. His head is shaved and he's got a goatee. He gives me a wave and a toothy grin.

I go into the library and look at the clock there. 8:05. The list is definitely up by now.

I wish I had shot better. I wish I had shot more. I replay all kinds of situations in my head that I should have done different. I look at the rack of new books. Mrs. Yost, the librarian, always puts out the new books on this wire rack for a month or so before she shelves them. I just stare at the covers. The words don't register.

Library clock says 8:07 now. The bell is going to ring. I've got to face up to it.

I walk as fast as I can toward the locker room. The list is definitely up. I stop at the door to get myself together. Slow my breathing down, smooth my hair, tuck in my shirt. I'm cool. Remember, I can always wrestle. Okay. I open the door.

There's a small knot of guys standing around the bulletin board: D-Man, Fred, Ziggy, Al, and Rudy. They turn when the door opens and look at me.

"You, man!" Rudy yells and he's pointing. His eyes look like they're going to bug out. They're all red like he's been crying or is about to.

I take a step back without even thinking. "What?"

"*You* took my spot!" He strides toward me. He's got on some kind of big-heeled, dopey, red, white, and blue shoes that make him look taller than he is. He gets all shrill. "Man, I *always* been on this team! Since eighth grade I been on this team!"

He looks like he might go for me. That doesn't worry me much except I don't want to get in trouble, and he looks a little crazy right now. He veers off from me, though, and starts stomping around, hitting lockers, and doing his tantrum thing till he finally slams the locker-room door open and bolts into the hall.

D-Man shakes his head. "Fool."

I walk up to the board. Al points to my name. "Are you, uh, Ray-mond Waz-now-ski?" He laughs and puts out a hand.

I slap him five. There it is. One sheet of white paper. Typed. Just a list with two headings: BOYS VARSITY BASKETBALL with a line under it. Then BOYS JUNIOR VARSITY BASKETBALL with a line under it. At the very bottom of the varsity list—Raymond Wisniewski.

I want to touch it, but everybody's there.

I feel a smile coming on, but I straighten it right out. Get neutral. No big deal. Made the team. Now other names come into focus. Demetrius Boyce, Zigmund Cryna, Raynell Floyd, Winston Harris, Alan Hayes, Stanley Pruzakowski, Robert Peyton, Richard Thomas. It's all about who I'd expected, except for me.

Bang! The hall door smashes open. Rudy comes running back in. I get my hands ready at my sides. Ready to come up. If he's going to get crazy with me, I'm going to defend myself. Left to block, right to punch.

He rushes right past me to the wall and he rips the list off the corkboard. The tacks go flying, spinning on the floor. He takes the list and tears it in half, then again, and again, all herky-jerky, like he can't control his hands.

Al yells, "Hey! You nuts?"

Rudy's crying with these little gasps. Then he throws all the bits of paper in the air like confetti. "Here's your BS list!"

We all stand there too stunned to even begin to figure what to do.

The coach's office door opens slowly and T leans out. He sees Rudy and Rudy sees him. Everything stops. Then Rudy turns and runs out of the locker room, slamming the door again.

T looks around and sees the list all over the floor in pieces. His face doesn't change, and he doesn't say anything. He goes back into his office. We're all still just standing there. I don't know if I should maybe help pick up the pieces.

In a second T comes back. He's got another copy of the list. He puts it right back up in the same place, nods at us, and closes the office door quietly behind him. The bell rings for first period. We all move out into the hall. Ziggy bumps me and says, "All right, Ray."

D and Al are laughing about Rudy. I'm just trying to hold back a smile. It's not about Rudy, though. I feel a little bad for Rudy. Not that I like Rudy, but I know what it feels like to be cut.

I'm fighting off this grin, because it's hitting me that I'm finally really on the team. I'm on the varsity! I earned my spot this year and I'm going to play. Finally! Thank you, God. All day I'm just floating.

When I get home from school I open the porch door and wipe my feet on the mat. Then I open the front door.

"Surprise!"

There are people yelling and cheering in my living room. Stoshy and Gerard are there and Stella, and my mom and my dad. Walter is right in front holding a pizza box in both hands and blowing one of those New Year's Eve horns in his mouth. He's blowing it over and over. Everybody's hugging me and shaking my hand and saying, "Congratulations!"

My dad claps me on the back. My mom says, "Walter called from school and told us. He went and got the pizza. I told him not to. I said I could have made something."

"No, this is great, Mom."

She whispers to me, "Is this going to be like that Stone team?"

"ROCK, Mom. Yeah, some of the guys are the same.

Pruze is on with me."

She smiles. "That's good that Stanley's there."

"Yeah, Mom." All I can do is smile and shake my head. She's just like I was when I first tried out. Glad there's another white guy around.

Finally Walter takes the horn out of his mouth. Actually Stella did it for him.

"All right, Ray! You de man! Number One B-Ball Scoring Machine! Mister Var-Si-Ty!" He's grinning and yelling. Walter's freckles spread all over his face. He puts the pizza box down and hugs me. When Walter hugs you, you understand what the term "bear hug" is all about. My ribs are touching.

With the breath I have left in me I tell him, "You're all right for a Polack."

"You de man, Ray! You de man!" he yells.

I say, "Hey, I thought you said b-ball is a bunch of crap."

My father turns on the radio. It's polka music. Big surprise.

Walter throws an arm around my neck, leans in, and says, "It is. I think you're sick in the head. But if you're into it, I'm there for you, man. I'm looking out for you."

And that's not a bad thing at all. A friend telling you he's there for you.

chapter eleven
DANCE PARTNERS

Our first game is against Northern Valley at home. T has me playing forward, and I'm totally psyched. I've been coming on the floor in practice as sixth man. I have been loving practice! It's been three weeks and I have loved every day of it. I love wearing the school-issued practice gear. I love the feel of the good-quality indoor balls. I've got a uniform. Number 44. I love playing with these guys. It's just like I hoped it would be. And now we're playing for real.

The game goes good. Actually, great. T puts me in at the eight-minute mark. The crowd is big, but it's not a problem. Just like ROCK. My concentration helmet flips down and all I can see is the court.

I inbound to Winnie and we go down. I go into the low post and Ziggy has the ball at the top of the key. I spring to the baseline and run my man into Larry. Ziggy hits me on the fly in the corner. My man is a step behind. I take the pass and go right up and shoot. The ball spins around and around and around the rim fast, like water going down a drain, and finally it's in! My first shot! My first basket!

I fly back to my defensive spot in the zone. It was kind of a weird shot, but it went in.

Ziggy slaps me five on the way to his spot and says, "Soft touch." After that one went in, the others come easy.

We win by five. I manage eight points and six rebounds. I also D up and hold my man to two buckets. I feel incredible. T shakes everyone's hand at the end. "Good game. Okay. Good thinking out there."

As we go into the locker room, this DJ table is getting set up while the adults and little kids file out. There's a dance in the gym tonight. I shower quick and get dressed. I'm dressed in a jacket and tie and good pants because that's what you have to wear on game days if you're on the team. T's rule.

Winnie comes over. He's wearing this gangster-looking pin-striped suit with a light purple tie and a shiny dark purple shirt.

"Hey," I say.

"Nice game." We slap five.

"I outscored you, though."

He makes a sour face. "Oh man, you scored that stuff on them slow Frankenstein forwards they got on North. Get out of here."

I have to laugh. "You stayin' for the dance?"

"Are you kiddin'?" He spreads his arms wide. "Like I'm going to disappoint all the ladies?"

The gym lights dim and these colored spotlights come on. It's like you're in a real cool place all of a sudden, not just the gym. "Love Train" by the O'Jays comes on, and the dance has started. It's soul oldies, which are cool. A cheerleader comes walking over. "Hey, boys. Nice game tonight."

Winnie says, "Hey, Bern. You met Ray?"

She is one of the two black cheerleaders. On our whole squad of twenty-six ballplayers, there's only three of us who are white. Meanwhile there are twelve cheerleaders and two are black. Figure that one out.

She's a little chunky for a cheerleader, but apparently can do whatever you have to do because she's on the squad. She puts a hand on her hip and tilts her head to the side. "Hi, Ray. I'm Bernadette." She smiles. "You guys looked good out there tonight."

I give her a smile back. "Thanks."

Winnie says, "Oh, hold on, there's my man Al, signaling me. Be right back."

Winnie goes over to where Al Hayes is waving at him. I wave to Al, too, and he gives me a salute. Bernadette and I are left standing there. I look around at the crowd under the colored lights. People all around us are dancing.

She starts bopping in place. "How do you like this music?" she asks.

"It's good."

She moves back and forth to the beat. "You dance?"

"Sometimes. A little."

"Well—?" She tilts her head at me and smiles. "You're really not going to make me dance by myself, are you?"

"Uh, no." I immediately start moving my feet.

I really hadn't planned on this. It's dark, though, which helps a lot. And Bernadette dances pretty regular, not like some girls where the whole gym would be staring at you.

At the end of the song, she goes right into the next one so I stay dancing, but then after that one it slows down. I'm not ready for a slow dance with Bernadette, so I say, "Let's take a breather over here."

We sit down on the bleachers and she says, "Having fun?"

"Yeah. Sure." I'm looking around. I can't say I'm totally comfortable with all this, but she seems really nice.

She pulls her hair back and puts a headband on. "You a friend of Winnie?"

"Yeah. How about you?"

She looks down and then to the side. "Oh, he's okay." And she laughs.

I tease her. "Oh, I get it. You wouldn't mind dancing a few with Winnie."

"Oh, you just a regular Houdini mind reader!"

I feel like I can trust Bernadette. She's one of these people you somehow know right away you can be honest with and they're not going to use it on you later. "Do you know Stacey?" I figure since they're both varsity cheerleaders she might be able to give me a clue or put in a word.

"Stacey Steck?"

"Yeah."

Bernadette holds up a hand like she's stopping traffic. "Don't bother. You're too nice. I can tell already."

"Come on. I'm not that nice. Really."

She laughs. "I'm serious."

"Stacey's all right."

She shrugs. "If you say so."

Not exactly the help I had hoped for. Might be she's a little jealous of Stacey. We're sitting there when Winnie comes back with D-Man. I scope out the place. Pruze is with Tommy Chessman and their girls. Nobody else is mixing it up. Like usual. All the whites are doing their thing together and all the blacks are doing their thing together except for me and Winnie and Pruze and Tommy C and Bernadette. Otherwise, it's like the lunchroom.

Winnie takes Bernadette out to dance. D-Man heads out with this other girl. I'm left standing there checking out the crowd. That's when I see Pina.

She's standing on the edge of the gym floor by herself, looking at her shoes. She looks up every few seconds and then back down. Her blond hair is back in a long ponytail. She's wearing a white dress with a big pink satin ribbon around the waist, black patent leather shoes, and little anklet socks. Her big, thick glasses reflect the colored lights. She's been in our neighborhood ever since I can remember. She's got Down's syndrome.

Even though she goes to a special class here, I've never seen her at a school social event before. Poor kid. She looks at her feet, then up again, then down. She hasn't moved an inch from that spot. People move around her like she's a rock in a stream.

Then from the crowd right behind her comes Stacey! And Walter. Stacey gently puts an arm across Pina's shoulder. Walter bends down. He's talking to Pina. She puts a little round fist up against her teeth. Walter takes her other hand and guides her slowly out onto the gym floor.

Walter holds Pina's right hand up and puts his arm around her waist and starts to dance. She follows him clumsily, giggling. Stacey stands on the edge of the floor, arms folded, watching and smiling.

Walter glances up and our eyes meet across the gym. I give him a thumbs-up, but he just looks back at Pina. Her steps are shuffly, but Walter keeps her going, and she starts to catch on so that they are making a square over and over. As they dance, a group of girls from Greenville clusters nearby. Pina can't stop grinning and giggling. At the end of the song, Walter bows and all the girls in the circle clap.

I work my way across the floor. I want to tell Walter it was cool what he did. I don't know if I would have done it even if I thought of it, but as I get closer I see him turn and head out into the crowd. Then Stacey sees me. Our eyes meet, and she gives me a little wave.

Whoah! She waved at me! I straighten my tie and feel for the cowlick. I take a deep breath and make my legs move forward. I'm feeling up and confident from the game. This could be my big chance.

The DJ is playing Kool and the Gang's "Jungle Boogie," which has really got a beat. I could dance to this. I have to yell over the music, "Hey, Stacey."

She smiles. "Hi, Ray. You like my matchmaking?"

I try to keep my voice steady. "That was awesome. Pina must by flying."

She shrugs. "I couldn't just leave her there like that. I mean, my god."

"That was really nice of you."

Stacey looks over my shoulder into the crowd while she's talking. "Oh, I've been doing things with Pina and the Association for Retarded Citizens for a couple of years. I got her here tonight."

"That's really cool."

"Yah. It's good for her." Then she puts up her hand for a high five. "Hey, nice game tonight, by the way."

I high-five her. "Thanks." Our hands touched!

"What's up, Stace?" It's the cheerleader captain, Hope. She comes up behind Stacey. She is a beautiful blond. Also very rich. I heard the only reason she goes to our school is she got kicked out of a couple of boarding schools.

Stacey gets all bubbly. "Hiya! Do you know Ray?"

Hope gives me a polite smile. "No. Hi."

We're standing there and Hope says, "You want to find Brock and Ryan?"

Stacey says, "Sure."

She's going to get away. The confident region in my brain says go for it. Quick. "Uh, Stacey. Before you go, you want to get in a dance?"

She winces. "Ooh. Sorry, Ray. Actually, I'm waiting for someone."

I automatically take a step back, but try to stay cool. "Oh, yeah. Okay. Well, catch you all later then."

She and Hope give me this high-pitched little "Bye!" together, and I give a weak wave.

I thread my way through the crowd. That stunk. That really stunk. As I walk away I hear them laughing these giggly girl-laughs. I look for Walter, but he's gone.

I scoop up my coat from the bleachers and just keep right on walking. I pass Winnie and Bernadette dancing by the sideline. I head out the door. I finally get up the guts to ask Stacey to do something and I crash and burn.

Well, at least I had a decent game.

chapter twelve
LITTLE HEAD/BIG HEAD

The next morning, I come downstairs to the smell of bacon. It's eight o'clock. I've got my sweats on because practice starts at nine. I walk into the kitchen and kiss my mom good morning.

"Do you want paska, Raymond?" she asks. Her hair's in curlers. She's got on her plaid apron.

"Yeah. Just one slice. Thanks, Mom." Paska is a sweet raisin bread. It's awesome toasted with butter. I could eat half a loaf, if I had time.

"How was your dance last night?" She's talking and cooking.

"It was okay. Hey, Dad."

He smiles and nods. "Raymond." He's got the paper open to the crossword puzzle.

"Did you meet any nice girls?" She stops and stares right at me when she asks. Then she looks away when I look back at her.

"Uh, yeah. Sure."

She wipes around the sink. My father looks up from the paper. "Vera."

My mother nods at my father. "I'm just asking if he met anyone at the dance. Here's your toast, honey." Mom puts the plate of paska down in front of me. There's already a glass of orange juice I've been sipping.

"Yep, Mom. Lots of kids were there."

She messes around some more by the sink and wipes the counters with a dishrag while I bite into the toast. "Walter's mother said you were dancing with a black girl."

I stop in midchew. I get up from the table and stuff the rest of the toast in my mouth.

"Vera!" My father is red.

"I'm just asking. It's just, I don't know, it's a surprise. We had those boys from basketball over to the house, but I didn't know he was going with black girls."

I put my plate in the sink. "Mom, I'm not 'going' with black girls."

My father says, "How about if we let him have a little privacy."

My mother gets quiet.

I gulp down the juice, then jump in to break the tension. I try to be casual. "I danced with one of the cheerleaders and she's black, yeah, but it's no big deal." I feel the red creeping up my neck as I head out of the kitchen.

My mother calls after me, "Mrs. Pieslak's daughter was there. Jeanine."

I call back, "Yeah. I just remembered. I gotta go and get some Gatorade for practice. I'll be right back."

As I get my jacket out of the hall closet, I hear my father say, "Why can't you leave him alone? He's seventeen, for crying out loud."

I close the front door and the argument dissolves into muffled words. I'm red-hot. And not at my mother. I jog over to 7-Eleven. I call Walter on the phone there.

He answers all sleepy, "Yeah?"

"Walter."

"Hey, my man Ray."

"Don't 'my man' me, you idiot. Meet me at the 7-Eleven."

"What? What time is it?"

"Never mind. Just meet me, you clown."

"All right, hold on to your business. When?"

"Now!"

He's awake now. "All right, all right. Give me ten minutes."

I hang out in front till Walter pulls up in the old blue pickup. "Hop in, buddy." He's all smiles. Big white teeth, freckles spread over a big face full of fun.

"You are such a jerk." I give him a good, hard rap in the arm as I hop in the front.

"What?" He looks at me, his eyebrows going up. He shuts the engine off.

I poke a finger in his chest. "Why did you tell your mother about me dancing with Bernadette?"

He smiles and knocks my hand away. "Who? That black girl? That was a secret? You danced with her in front of the whole school."

"Yeah. Kids. Not your mother. Not *my* mother."

Walter reaches into his pocket and pulls out some gum. He slips a stick out and flips it to me, then jams one in his own mouth. "Look, I just mentioned it. My mother asked about you, and I just mentioned it."

I give him a bad look, but unwrap the gum and fold the stick into my mouth. "Well, don't mention that kind of stuff."

He grins and leans on top of the steering wheel. "What stuff shouldn't I mention? When you do things with black people?"

"You know what I mean, idiot boy. You want me to start telling my parents about some of the stuff you do?"

Walter relaxes, now that he knows what it's all about. He lays back against his door and puts his feet up on the dashboard. "Look. You know why you're upset? Huh? Because you're embarrassed. You were dancing with a black girl. What's that about?"

"I danced with her once because she asked me. Big deal! And what's with you anyway? I saw you there, I know you saw me, and you skipped right out."

"What was I gonna do? Hang with you and your special friends?"

"Now you're going to tell me who to hang with?"

Walter pauses and takes a deep breath. "Look. I know

you're into the b-ball thing and you gotta play with these savages. But who says you have to dance with them and hang out with them?"

My stomach flips when he says it. "Knock it off."

"What?"

"You know what."

Walter snorts. He shakes his head and looks at me for a few seconds like he's trying to see into my head. Finally he says, "You do what you want, but I'm telling you, it don't look good."

I'm definitely going to be late for practice now. He's serious and the whole thing is stupid. I open my door and get out. Then I slam it shut and stick my head back in the window. "Walter, I don't care what it looks like." I glance at my watch. I've got to get going. "Bottom line. *Do not* keep telling people, especially your mother, about what I'm doing. You got that, stupid Polack?"

Walter smiles just a little. Calling him "stupid Polack" is like a term of endearment to him. He looks at me for a second. "Okay. Telling my mother, maybe that wasn't a . . . uh . . . good choice. Like they say in guidance."

"You got that right."

"My bad. It won't happen again." He puts out his hand for a shake. I take it. "You want to be a private person? No problem. But, Ray . . . "

"Yeah?"

He holds on to my hand. "Don't try to tell me how to talk about people."

I feel my shoulders tighten up.

Walter squints at me, my hand still stuck in his grip. "I'm just jokin' around, right?"

"Yeah. Right." He finally lets go.

We both stare at each other. Nothing to say. I don't want to leave this totally negative. "Anyway. That was cool, what you did last night, dancing with Pina."

Walter shrugs. "What can I say? I take care of my own." He starts up the truck, then yells over the rattling engine. "Hey, Ray!"

I back off the truck, "Yeah?"

He's leaning toward me grinning. "Next time? Try Jeanine Pieslak. I hear she gives."

"Get lost, Walter."

He smiles so big you can see his gums. He beeps the horn, guns the engine, and moves the truck quick back onto the road. I run home to get my gym bag.

Because of my "little talk" with Walter, I am late for practice and have to do ten laps at the end. Saturday practices are optional for T to call or not. It may be sick, but I'm glad when he does. I love practice. I love playing, period.

Walking home from practice I think about what Walter said this morning. It was not a good conversation. And why was I so nervous about my mother hearing about me dancing with Bernadette anyway?

When I get home I see my dad in the garage under the van.

I call, "Hey, Dad, I'm home. You need a hand under there?"

"No, thanks. I'm just finishing up. I'm coming out." He scoots out from underneath. "How was practice?" he asks.

"Good."

He starts putting stuff away. Hanging up the oil filter wrench, the ratchet, the funnel. He has Peg-Board all over the garage with metal hooks for everything. The screwdrivers are in order by size and type. My mom's the same way with her stuff.

As he moves around with the tools he says, "You know, I wanted to talk to you a little about your involvement with girls."

"Yeah?" Oh geez. Now he's going to start in about Bernadette.

He leans on the workbench and starts cleaning his hands with a rag. "Well, I mean I know you had all those classes in school." He's looking at me real directly. He's not shy or anything.

"Yep."

"There's just one thing."

Here it comes. Here comes the black thing.

"My father told me this and it's still true." He stops moving the rag. "With girls, never let your little head do your thinking for your big head. That's how you get in trouble."

I'm a little stunned. I feel a smile starting, but tuck that away fast. "Yeah. Okay."

He nods. "Okay, then."

chapter thirteen
PARTY AT HECTOR'S

Walter slumps down with his head on the cafeteria table at lunch. "Man, I got to get some sleep. Stella just won't let me be."

Stoshy shakes his head. "What is wrong with that picture?"

Gerard takes a sip of chocolate milk. "A lot."

Walter laughs and raps me on the shoulder. "How about you, man? You getting it on? Still hot for Stacey?"

"Everybody with a pulse is hot for Stacey, Walter."

Walter says, "You know. I think she's just playing hard to get."

It's good to hear Walter talking in a friendly way. It's been a little quiet between us since we had the talk about the dance. But I think Stella makes him feel really good just in general. I roll my eyes. "Yeah, you know a lot about it."

He punches me, grinning. "I'm the master. Just ask Stella."

Stoshy looks like he's starting to grow a mustache. He

smooths it with his fingers. "I have to fight them off."

Gerard says all deadpan, "So far you've been real success-
ful there."

I say, "Nothing's gonna happen sitting around watching
Dr. Shock."

"Oh, man! Just like you, right? By the way, where is
Stacey? Are you lunching together?" Stoshy raises his eyebrows at me.

Gerard says, "When's the last time you did a *Dr. Shock*
hang anyway? We could watch the movie, then head out and
pick up the wild women. We don't see you around anymore,
man."

I shrug. "Games are Tuesdays and Fridays. You could
have taped it and we could have watched it another night."

"Nah. It's not the same," Gerard mumbles. He's eating a
big bag of Fritos.

I take a slug of orangeade. "Oh, yeah. What is it, like
pay-for-view?"

Walter messes up Gerard's hair. "Hey. Get off Ray-Ray's
case. He's still de man. I can't do Fridays anyway because of
the stand. So we'll just do it another night."

"Yeah," I say. But nobody says anything about what night
it might be.

I line up in the circle for the tap. T is letting me start and
jump center! Me, Winnie, Robert, Al, and Pruze. T made me
a starter in practice. A varsity starter!

I shake hands with the center from Warren Hills. I recognize him from the PAL league and right away I feel good because I know I can handle him. I did it last year.

The concentration helmet is on and everything is cool. I love being on this court. I've got a good rhythm on the floor. I make my outside shots. Get some rebounds. Play good D. In fact, we all look good and we win by ten. This is our third win in a row. It's no harder than ROCK ever was.

It's definitely easier to play a game than to get through a practice with Coach T. His practices are bust-your-butt, flat-out killers. In between torture sessions, while we're sitting on the sideline gasping for air, in his real calm voice he says, "Conditioning. When it comes down to it, to the last seconds, to the overtime, to the last shot, to the press, it's who's in condition that's going to win it. You will be in condition."

That's for sure. We will be in condition or we will be in the cemetery. But he's not just running us, he's teaching us. We run three different zones and have like ten set plays we can work off of.

At the buzzer, Winnie comes over and bumps me. "Nice game, Ray. You weren't half bad."

"You weren't neither, when you weren't hogging the ball."

"What? Somebody got to put points on the board."

Robert walks by without a glance at us. He was high scorer with twenty points, but he took a lot of shots to get his twenty. Pruze comes over and drapes his big arms around me and Winnie. We head into the locker room together. "Nice win. Nice win. We beat a bunch of farmers, but at least it's a win. We're gonna have a great season, I'm tellin' ya. You boys goin' over to Hector's party? Celebrate a little?"

Winnie says, "No. I got to be home tonight."

Pruze sits on a bench and starts rubbing that stinky Atomic Balm on his legs. "How about you, superstar? You going?"

Hector is a guy in my gym class. He's supposed to be a real partyer. "I don't know. I didn't hear anything about it."

Pruze tilts his head at me, his long blond hair falling in his eyes. He parts it down the middle so he can see me. "Yes you did. I just told you. You need a ride?"

"I don't know."

"What do you mean, you 'don't know'? Like you don't know if you're going or you don't know if you need a ride?"

"Uh." I figure I'll goof on Pruze. "I don't know."

He throws a sock at me, but I'm already ducking. "C'mon, man. You never go to this stuff. Just check it out. You know, Stacey is definitely going to be there. You go to this party, things could happen."

That gets my attention, but I keep goofing. "I never go because nobody ever asks."

Then he does a pretty good imitation of a girl. "Raymond, please come with me to Hector's party. It would be so special."

"Well, okay. You deserve a break."

Pruze flips back to his normal Chicago voice, "Yeah, right. I'll pick you up in an hour."

Pruze is always going out somewhere to a party. I feel kind of nervous about it. I know there's going to be some drinking, maybe drugs. But if Stacey is there . . . Anyway, I'm just going to check it out.

The other nervous thing is, Hector lives in Jefferson Park. So it's not just a jock party, which is a new thing to me, but a party at night in Jefferson Park.

Pruze picks me up an hour later in his old, pale yellow Cadillac Sedan DeVille. It's a huge tank, covered with rust and patch paint, but—it's a car. He's got the radio blasting so we can hear it over the engine and he's singing along. We stop on the way to pick up Ziggy. Three white boys going to a party in Jefferson Park.

We find the house on a street that's hardly a street. It's not even paved. The house is small, but with sections that are added on in funny ways, with different kinds of siding. Like somebody just kept saying, hey, we need another room here, so they tacked it on. Pruze bops with his head and sings, "In the ghetto—" It's an Elvis song that you always hear on these oldies stations. Me and Ziggy crack up. It breaks the tension a little.

Cars are everywhere. Even in the yard. We park around the corner. You can hear music from the house, and we're a block away. Pruze winks at me. "Hector knows how to party!"

We tiptoe through this muddy lawn to an orange front

door. I've never seen anything orange on a house before, let alone the front door. Pruze doesn't knock or anything. No one would hear us. He just opens the door, and walks right in. Me and Ziggy follow right behind. There's no hall, it's just—boom! You're standing in the living room.

A couple of guys have to move over to get us in and close the door. Kids are everywhere, lined up against the paneled walls, sitting on the floor, standing around. Everybody's got a beer bottle or a can or something. On the right is a couch and on the left is the kitchen, all lit up with greenish fluorescent lighting.

I smell dope. I immediately start to feel tight. My shoulders go up like when I'm cold. Pruze is smiling. He yells across the room, "Hey Tommy C."

Tommy Chessman yells back, "Hey, hey, hey!"

He squeezes through the crowd and comes over. He's got on a Knicks jersey and jeans. His head is grazing the hanging lamp in the middle of the ceiling.

The living room is crammed with people and stuff, beanbag chairs, the couch, a big-screen TV that's got on some game show. There's no sound coming out of the TV or if there is, you can't hear it.

"Hey, Pruze! Ziggy! And my man, Ray!" Tommy bumps us all and yells loud into the kitchen, "Hey, Hector, man, the Polacks is here!"

Hector comes waddling out into the living room. He's a big, round Puerto Rican guy. His eyes are like slits. He's wearing an undershirt and gym shorts. "Hey, wha's goin' on? Come on, get a beer. Throw your coats on the bed here."

We follow him into this tiny, messy bedroom next to the kitchen and put our coats on a huge pile. At the kitchen table there's a man in a white T-shirt with his sleeves rolled up, laughing, smoking a cigarette, and drinking a beer with all these girls around him.

"*Chicas*, I gotta tell you. I gotta tell you." He pounds the table. "It was soooo beautiful. *Bonita! Bonita!* It was soooo beautiful. I canna' tell you. I canna' tell you!"

"Hey, Pops, man, cool out," Hector says. He reaches in the fridge and comes out with three cans of beer.

"What, cool out? I'm hot, man. I'm a hot potato!" The man laughs this crazy laugh with his head back, his nose pointing at the ceiling. The girls all giggle.

Hector ignores him and hands us each a cold beer.

"Your old man is something else," Pruze says.

"Yeah." Hector takes a swig of beer.

It's his father! Unbelievable.

I look into the living room. My eyes are adjusting to the dark, and there's Robert and Rudy. As usual they're together. They're sitting on the floor in the living room leaning up against the wall looking at me. Each has a beer. I look away.

Pruze and Tommy C squeeze in on a couch. I sit on half the arm and Ziggy leans on the other half near me. Tommy takes something out of his jeans pocket and lights it. It's a joint. He takes a big drag and passes it to Pruze.

Oh, geez. I don't mind that people do dope and stuff, I just don't like to be this close to it. I'm not even crazy about the fact that I'm sitting here with a beer. I figure I better open it and take a sip or look dumb sitting with it in my hand. I've never liked beer much, but at least I won't look too out of it.

Pruze leans over and yells, "Hey, bro, want a hit?" He holds the joint out for me.

I shake my head and yell back, "No, man. I got my beer."

He shrugs, "Suit yourself. More for us."

"You got it," Tommy C says, giggling.

I get up. I figure I'll walk around. Ziggy slides over and takes my spot and grabs his turn on the joint. This is the most brothers and others I've ever seen together in one place. I guess dope and drink bring people together. There are plenty of guys from the football team and lots of girls. Cheerleaders. Everybody who's cool.

I walk over to the next room and poke my head around the corner and there's Stacey! Sitting on a couch. She looks so good my heart jumps. Right next to her, though, is this football dude I've seen around, Brock Janson. She turns to him and he says something in her ear. Next to them is Hope and our quarterback, Ryan Ford. They are all entwined in each other. I scoot right out of the room. I was hoping she'd be here, but not with some huge jock whispering in her ear.

I don't want to hang around Pruze smoking the dope. I don't want to watch Stacey and the football dude, and I don't want to go back in the kitchen with Hector's crazy father. So why am I still here? I go to the bedroom, get my coat, and head out the back door so I won't have to explain about leaving.

The night air smells crisp and clean after all that smoke-and-beer smell. And then I start to run. I don't feel comfortable just walking around Jefferson Park in the middle of the night, so I run till I get to the high school and then walk on home. It's a long run.

When I come in the door my mom and dad are sitting reading the papers. Actually my mom is sleeping in her chair with the papers in her lap. "How was your party?" Dad asks.

"Okay."

"Walter called."

"Oh yeah? What'd he say?"

"He said he wanted to get together. He got tonight off. I told him you were at a party."

"Thanks, Dad. Good night."

It's only ten o'clock. There's still a half hour left of *Dr. Shock*.

chapter fourteen
DEFINITELY NO PROBLEM

"What does it take to win your love for me?" It's Monday morning in the cafeteria and I'm running that old Jr. Walker and the All Stars song in my head. I love oldies. I like polkas, too, so maybe my musical tastes are a little out of step.

"What's up?" Walter flops down in the chair across from me, morning Coke in hand.

"Nothing. How about you? You're late."

"Sorry, Mom. Had to wee."

"How many times do I have to tell you, go before you leave the house."

"Yeah." He grins. "Hey. Heard you went to a party."

"Yeah."

"Where at? I didn't hear about no party."

"It was at this Hector kid's house."

Walter shakes his head and stares. "Doesn't he live down in that damn ghetto?"

"It's not a ghetto."

"Right. It's Disney World."

Here we go again. I'm having to explain things to Walter like I got caught doing something wrong. I feel a little heat growing in my chest. "I went with Ziggy and Pruze. A lot of guys from the team were there. Get off my case."

I figure he's going to start again about who I'm hanging with, but he just stares. Then he shrugs. "Whatever."

The bell rings. We get up, neither one of us saying anything. We round the corner into the hall. "Catch you at lunch," I say as I split off.

Walter raises a hand and waves, then melts into the crowd. I'm mad, but the heat drains out of my chest when he walks away without talking. I want to say something like, "We're still friends, right?" Like I'm five years old again.

At practice I warm up with some turnaround jumpers from the baseline. The turnaround is a nice shot, and it's funny because I don't even see the basket, but it's a high percentage shot for me. Sometimes it seems like if I can't see what I'm doing, if I just go totally by feel, it works better.

I do a turnaround, land, and there's Rudy walking into the gym with Malovic. I haven't seen Rudy in here since the last day of tryouts. Then he points at me. Malovic glances over. What is that about?

They walk over to Coach T's office. Malovic knocks and then they both go in and close the door behind them. I walk up to Pruze. "Hey. Did you see Rudy and Malovic go into T's office?"

Pruze shrugs. "No. Maybe Rudy left his hair gel here and Malovic came to help him find it."

"Rudy was pointing at me."

Pruze dribbles the ball through his legs and behind his back. He's pretty good with the ball for a big guy. "Malovic was probably giving him some kind of IQ test. You know, point to something bigger than a bread box."

"I don't know. I don't like it."

"Forget it."

Practice starts, but I'm off. Why would Rudy be in there with Coach T and Malovic? And why would he be pointing at *me*?

We run some scrimmages and that helps get my mind off it a little. We finish up with sprints and start walking out.

"Raymond. Stanley."

I feel a chill all over me. I look at Pruze. He's looking at T. "Yeah, Coach?" he says.

"Shower up and meet me in my office in ten minutes, please." He turns and walks into the locker-room.

Ten minutes later we're sitting with wet hair on two plastic cafeteria chairs in the gym office. Coach sits opposite us in his chair, his legs wide apart.

"At the beginning of practice today Mr. Malovic and Rudy Robinson came here to tell me about a party that you two might have attended over the weekend. Were you at a party?"

That's what it is! Oh, man, we're in trouble. What are we going to say? I watch Pruze for a clue.

"Yeah," says Pruze. I nod yes.

"Was it at a Hector Garces's house?"

"Yes, sir." says Pruze.

"Yes, sir," I echo. I'm trying to decide what to do with my face. Should I smile? Look grim? Concerned?

"And was Rudy there?" T is sitting straight up in his chair. No expression. Not mad. Not happy.

"Yeah, he was there," says Pruze.

I just nod.

"Were either of you in violation of training rules? Using alcohol or drugs?" He says it like he's just interested. Like, "Do you floss?"

Pruze, looking like a choir boy, says, "No way."

"No, sir." I say. I'm sticking with the sirs on this. My heart is banging on my chest.

"Rudy indicated you were both smoking marijuana and that Robert Peyton would corroborate this."

My heart is now like a runaway train. I try to stay still. Pruze looks to me, like it's my turn to pitch in. I don't. Pruze shrugs. "He doesn't like us."

Coach puts his hands together. His arms are big under the golf shirt. He leans back in his chair. "Any reason?"

Pruze looks to me again. I don't know what to say so he keeps going. "Well, he's real mad at Ray because he thinks Ray took his spot on the team."

T doesn't say anything for a second. Then he tilts his head. "Why did he accuse you too then, instead of just Raymond?"

This time Pruze takes a second. Then he says, "Like I said, he thinks Ray took his spot, but he and Robert— I don't like to say it, but they don't like white guys."

Coach doesn't react. I'm thinking that's a hard thing to say to a black man, but Pruze is pretty honest, except for keeping his butt out of trouble.

"Do you agree with that, Raymond?"

I figure what else can it be? I never did anything to either one of them. "I guess. Yeah."

Coach doesn't say anything. His eyes are still on me. His big thick eyebrows look kind of worried.

I look down.

"Thank you, gentlemen," Coach T says. He's up, showing us to the door.

"Okay, Coach. No problem," says Pruze.

"We'll talk more about this tomorrow," he says.

Me and Pruze walk out of the gym and into the hall. "What do you think?" I whisper.

Pruze pulls on his coat and answers me in a normal voice. "Nobody's going to be able to prove anything, so we're totally cool. Like I said, don't sweat it."

I can't believe how cool he is. "What if he suspends us?"

He rolls his eyes. "C'mon, Ray. Because some nutcase like

Rudy says he saw you smoking dope? You didn't even do it, remember?"

I take my gym bag and slide it down the hall like a bowling ball. Try to show Pruze I'm cool. "Yeah, okay."

Pruze says, "Besides, it was a great party. Hector does know how to party!"

"Are you talking about Hector's?" It's a girl voice behind us.

Pruze and I spin around. Stacey is there with her gym bag over her shoulder. Our eyes meet. Those green eyes are amazing. They look like they're lit up with something. I blurt, "Hi. Stacey." It comes out sounding like I did when I was twelve.

"Hi, Ray," she says. "Hi, Stanley."

Pruze bows. "Stacey."

She has on a white V-neck sweater and a khaki skirt riding high on her thighs. She's stopped and is talking to me right here in the hall! She says, "I saw you there, right? At Hector's?"

Stacey is talking to me! "Yeah. Pruze and some of the guys from the team were going so I went."

Pruze says, "Yes. I invited Raymond. I was unable to secure a date of the opposite gender so he was the next best thing."

I punch him and he runs down the hall. Stacey laughs, watching him scamper away. "You know. I'm glad you're on varsity this year. That's so cool."

"Yeah. It's really . . . uh, well . . . good."

"My. You really have a way with words, young man."

I have to laugh. "Well, yeah: 690 on my Verbal."

"Really?" She looks interested. "What's your class rank?"

"Top ten-twenty percent, I hope. That's what I need to get into State. How about you?"

She starts to walk a little, so I follow. "I'm number two right now, but Maryanne Pinelli has AP Calculus this semester, so I've got a good shot at number one by the time everything wraps up."

"Wow." That basically sums up how I feel about everything about Stacey.

"Don't be impressed. You're probably like two-tenths of a grade point behind me." She hugs her books to her chest and flips her hair back. "Did you have a good time at Hector's? I saw you and then you were gone."

She noticed! She was looking for me? Thinking about me? I shrug. "Yeah. It was okay."

She nods. "I know. I'm not into the drinking and everything, but all my friends were there so—"

"Same with me." I am amazed. We are connecting!

"Well, I'm going to go get some homework done." She gives me a great smile. "I don't want Maryanne gaining any ground."

"All right. Have a good day." Ouch! Have a good day! How lame is that? As soon as it's out of my mouth, I want to kick myself. She waves and jogs out to the parking lot.

I just had a conversation with Stacey! And even though I talked like an idiot, I get the feeling there might be something there.

Pruze waits for me by the door with my gym bag. He nods toward the parking lot and elbows me in the side. "See. I told ya. You go to these parties and things happen."

"Yeah, like we get thrown off the team."

Pruze shakes his head. "Trust me. That is definitely no problem."

chapter fifteen
TOUGH POLACK GUYS

I wish I could be more like Pruze. I spend most of the night and the next day worrying, but when I mention it to him, he just says nothing's going to happen. T doesn't say a thing about it during practice, but right after we go in the locker room he pokes his head in and says, "Raymond. Stanley."

Here it comes.

"In here for a minute please. You don't have to change. It won't take long."

Pruze bobs his head. "Okay, Coach."

We walk through the door together. There's Rudy and Robert sitting in two cafeteria chairs. There are two empty ones opposite those. We shoot quick looks at each other and then me and Pruze sit in the empty chairs. The office is small and our knees are all almost touching. Rudy and Robert are dressed alike with blue work pants, knit sweaters, and big hiking boots. They look like strange twins. Like a circus act or something.

Coach closes the door and sits down on the edge of his

desk. His face is just cool. No sign of anything. "Gentlemen, I wanted you all here together to hear the final word on this. And I will be brief." He runs his eyes over each of us. "Clearly I was not present at the party in question, but I can still offer a few observations." He nods to himself. "Whatever your actual individual involvement with drugs or alcohol may have been, you all know you made a mistake."

"Huh? What mistake?" Rudy is just talking right out as usual. I shoot him a disgusted look.

"All of you claim not to use drugs or alcohol and yet you were all present at a party where you admit there was under-age drinking and illicit drug use. That was very poor judgment on everyone's part and very suspect as well."

Rudy is squinting at Coach. "Say what?"

Robert stares straight ahead at the wall.

"Stay away from trouble. That's what it means, Rudy. I need to reinforce the importance of staying out of compromising situations like this party. So, two things are going to happen."

Coach pushes off the desk and stands up. "You are all going to run ten laps each day before practice this week and you are going to spend an hour under my supervision picking up trash around the school grounds, which you will quickly find is mostly empty beer cans and bottles. We will turn these in for recycling. You may choose not to participate, but should you do so, you will be off the team. Any questions?"

Nobody's saying anything. Then Rudy says kind of cautiously, like he's not sure if he's going to get slammed for it, "I ain't doin' this. I ain't even on the team."

T just stays real still. Only his lips move. "That's fine. You may go."

Rudy squeezes out of his chair and stands up. "What about Robert? He didn't do nothing. He was just being a witness."

Robert keeps staring at the wall. T answers, "He was also at the party so the consequences are the same."

Rudy looks at Robert. Robert isn't moving. Rudy's mouth opens and closes, but nothing comes out. This was obviously not working out the way he figured. He finally tosses his head and pimp rolls out.

"Laps start tomorrow before practice. Trash pickup begins tomorrow morning at six."

Pruze chokes, "Six!"

Coach's lips form something that's almost a smile. "Will that interfere with your paper route, Stanley?"

"Uh, no."

"Fine. I'll see you three tomorrow morning at the front entrance at six." He walks us out the door. "Also, you need to be aware, I have informed all of your parents this afternoon, so they will understand why you are involved in these extra commitments."

I stop. He called our parents! I mumble, "My father's gonna kill me."

T pats my back. "That's fine, Raymond. Shows you he cares."

When I walk in our front door, my father is waiting for me, in his work clothes. My mom doesn't allow him anywhere in the house with his work clothes on, but here he is on the carpet, in the living room, with his work boots. He greets me with, "What the hell were you thinking going to a party with dope and booze?"

"Dad, I didn't know for sure there was going to be anything at the party till I got there."

He shakes his head and puts an arm behind his neck. He drops it and walks back and forth again. "It was in Jefferson Park, wasn't it?"

"Yeah, but—"

"You didn't tell us you were going to Jefferson Park."

"Dad, I went there with Pruze and Ziggy. It's not a big deal. Besides, I was there ten minutes. I saw what was going on and I left right away."

He stops and takes a breath. He put his hands on his hips and looks at me. Then he asks in a normal voice, "That's what happened?"

"That's it."

"You didn't smoke anything?"

"*No*. Dad, come on."

"Were you drinking?"

How to answer that one? "Not exactly."

He flares up. "Don't bullshit with me, Raymond!"

"I opened a beer. I took a sip. I just opened it because—you know, everyone else had one."

He gets quiet. He walks to the window and looks out, rubbing the bald spot on the back of his head. He doesn't say anything for a long time. "I don't know. I don't know about this basketball and parties and you with all these black kids."

"Dad, you work with black guys."

He automatically says, "That's different."

I mumble. "It's not different."

A lot of fathers would just yell and tell you to shut up. Maybe whack you. He looks around, like for words, and then sighs. "Raymond, those are adults I've worked with for a long time. They're not . . . It's different."

He turns his back on me, then sits down on the couch. I just stand there. We both stare into space for a bit. Finally he motions to the spot next to him. He exhales hard. It seems like all the mad is going out of him. I sit down.

"Raymond, you're scaring me."

I just look.

"You're scaring the crap out of me."

He stops and blinks. "I didn't think you would ever in a million years be involved with stuff like this. And then your coach called and I couldn't believe it."

I feel like a total jerk. "I know. I shouldn't have gone, but I didn't know exactly what it was going to be like, and I wanted to check it out. When I found out, I left and that's the truth. I was home by ten Friday, remember?"

He nods. And then nods again, looking at the carpet.

Finally he taps me on the shoulder. "Okay, Raymond. Okay." He exhales hard again. "And forget what I said about your black friends. That was kind of stupid. It just seems to me you were never in trouble and now all of a sudden you're in trouble. What I mean is, stay away from people who can get you into trouble."

"Yeah. Don't worry, Dad." Not a lot of parents are going to admit they told you something stupid. But, there it is.

He looks at a spot behind me on the wall. "I'm always going to worry, Raymond. That's part of being a parent. It's just that I—we don't want to see you hurt."

We? "Dad, does Mom know about this?"

He chuckles. "No. Miracle of miracles—she wasn't home to take the call. I got it. I think maybe God wanted to save us all that aggravation. I don't think she needs to know about it."

"Yeah. Thanks, Dad."

"No use everybody having heart attacks."

"No."

He stands up and then I do. "Hey, Dad."

"Yeah?"

"I'm sorry."

He gives me a hug and I give it right back. Tough Polack guys can do that.

As long as no one else is watching.

chapter sixteen
TUTORIAL

The sky is still dark when Pruze and I get to school for our first bottle-and-can pickup session. It's cold and damp and all the stuff is slimy and wet. We don't say much. Pruze grunts a lot, though, when he bends over, but that's about it. I'm real surprised when I see Robert show up. I thought he'd figure a way out of it or just diss Coach and blow it off, but he's here.

T just watches us and sometimes writes in a notebook he has. When we finish at seven a.m., he puts the garbage bags full of recyclables in his trunk, says, "Thank you," gets in his car, and drives off. He came over to the school just for that. I heard he still teaches PE at Bridgeton High School for his regular job.

After we're done I go to the cafeteria and crash. I'm staring at nothing when big hands cover my eyes. I grab the wrists and push, but the hands press firmer against my face.

"Guess who?"

I finally manage to twist under and out, stand up, and

pull Walter's paws off me. "What are you doing?" I'm a little annoyed. I don't much like it when he tries to muscle me like that in front of people. I straighten my hair out.

"Nothing, man. Checking your vision." He's grinning.

"My vision's fine, you ape." I hit him one in the arm, but he's wearing a big wool coat so he probably doesn't even feel it.

Walter pulls back and throws a jab in the air near my head. I throw three quick jabs with an open hand and touch his face with each one to show him I'm still quicker than him. Then I sit down. Walter does the same. He pops his Coke open and starts rocking from side to side. "So what's new?" he says. He's in a weird mood, like giddy.

"Well, I had a conversation with Stacey yesterday."

He pops his eyes. "No way. About what?"

"You know. Stuff."

"Like where and when and how long?" he says smiling.

"No. Not quite yet."

He puts his feet up on a chair. "I heard your butt is in trouble because of that great party you had to go to."

I don't say anything. He shakes his head. "I don't want to say I told you so. But look at what's goin' on since you've been doin' your black-guy hang. You're the only white guy I know doing this stuff."

The heat rises up in my chest. "What are you talking about? The place was packed with white guys *and girls*. Like Stacey. I went over there with Ziggy and Pruze."

"Ziggy and Pruze are potheads."

"Oh, please, Mr. Clean."

Walter leans forward. "Ray. Look. I'm just giving you some advice."

"You're going to give me advice?"

The bell rings and we get up. I walk over to the stairwell because I'm going up. I stop and point a finger at him. I want to make sure he gets the message. "Walter. I don't want to hear any more about this from you. Capisce? Can it."

He puts up his hands like he's surrendering. He smiles and the freckles spread all over his face. "Hey. You say stop. I stop. You say go. I go."

I don't smile. I want him to get it. "I'm serious."

"What did I say? I said I'm stopped, right? What do you want, a contract?"

"Yeah. All right."

"All right then. Catch you at lunch." He keeps smiling that big goofy grin. It's like, under it all, he's glad my butt is in trouble.

The ten laps are a pain, but that's just the way it is. We're running them while the other guys are warming up. It's hardest on Pruze. He hates to run. Robert is doing the whole deal without talking or even looking at me or Pruze. Like he's too good for us.

Practice is okay even with the laps and by Friday I'm feeling pretty good, because we're through all that and I've really been hitting my jumper this week. I'm on one of those streaks where you shoot and ask yourself, why would it miss? And it doesn't.

At the end of practice Coach T calls me over to the bleachers. "Raymond."

I jog over and stand there looking down at him. "Yeah, Coach?" Maybe he wants to talk about some kind of play to free me up for the jumper.

"Sit down, Raymond."

Not a good tone. He sounds tired. I sit down and I'm thinking what is this about? I hope it isn't more about the party.

Coach looks straight and tall even when he's sitting down. His chest swells out the golf shirt. "Raymond, you have many attributes that are important for a good varsity player. You really have a great deal of potential."

"Thanks, Coach." The stuff about "important attributes" is an incredible compliment. The "potential" thing scares me. When teachers and coaches talk about your potential they mean you have something on the ball, but you haven't done anything about it yet.

"However, you're still struggling with your ballhandling." He smiles slightly when he says it, probably so I won't be real offended. I know it's kind of true. I don't have to dribble much in my position.

"I guess." I nod. Now what?

"No need to guess, Raymond. Your ballhandling needs work. It's inadequate for a starting player."

"Okay." I need to work on something. But he said "starting" player. Am I going to lose my starting spot?

"We need to see significant improvement in this area." He lets that hang there with his eyes on me. I already said okay. What was I supposed to say now? The silence starts to get deafening.

"I'm going to provide you with a tutor for ballhandling."

A tutor? Maybe this is not a bad thing. "Okay."

"Your recycling work and laps are finished so you will have time to begin next week. You are going to train every day after practice with the tutor for half an hour."

Coach amazes me, the way he makes you do stuff like the recycling and now this tutorial. I nod again. My eyes are starting to burn from staring back at him to show him I'm paying attention.

"Robert will begin the tutorial sessions with you Monday."

"Robert!" My throat tightens up. "He's the tutor?"

"Yes."

"Does he know that?"

"Not yet, but he will."

I don't like to risk telling Coach anything he doesn't want to hear, but this is too much.

"Coach. Maybe I could do this with someone else? Like Winnie. He's a good ball handler."

Coach stands up. "No. Remain after practice on Monday to begin working out with Robert."

I've got to say something. I can't deal with Robert being my personal coach. "Coach, I don't know if this would actually work out real well."

He doesn't even blink. "Raymond. You will *make* it work." He smiles slightly.

All I can manage is a nod. But I do it twice.

"Have a good weekend, Raymond." Then he walks that real straight-up walk back to his office.

I'm hoping maybe Coach will change his mind. But Monday after practice ends, sure enough, he tells me and Robert to stay and wait on the bench for him. Pruze looks back as he goes into the locker room. He makes devil horns on his head at me.

After everybody clears out, T comes back from his office with a piece of paper. "Gentlemen. You will work together for half an hour. Just follow the drills listed here." He holds the paper out to Robert. "Robert, you will—"

Robert cuts in, in his low croaky voice. "I got homework."

T still has his hand extended with the paper in it. His expression doesn't change. It looks like he's just waiting at a corner for the light to change. Not mad. Not happy. Just waiting.

Finally, he lowers his arm and says, "You need to apologize for interrupting."

Robert curls his lip and stands up. He takes half a step.

T is looking at the paper. "Robert. If you leave this room, you are off the team and you are not coming back. If you show that level of disrespect, you don't belong here."

Robert glowers, but he stops. You can almost see the struggle busting out in his head. He knows he can't run this BS on Coach T like he did Malovic. It seems like an hour, but he finally swallows it and sits down again, no expression on his face. T looks at him. "I'm waiting," he says. There's no off-the-hook here.

You can barely hear Robert spit it out. "Sorry."

T picks right up again with his talk. "Fine. If you have any homework difficulties, see me. I will be more than glad to help out in that department. Now, follow the schedule. Do not deviate from it. Robert, I am depending on you to lead the tutorial properly." He hands Robert a ball and the paper and walks back to his office. All you can hear are his sneakers. Tap, tap, tap. Across the floor.

I can't help but give Robert a dig. I stand up, stretch my arms out, look around the gym, and say, "Glad to hear you're sorry."

He growls, "You lucky I don't go upside your head."

Most Robert has ever said to me. I look at the ceiling. "Anytime, man. And by the way. That was real good. You put eight words together in a row by yourself."

His eyes widen and he looks like he might come after me. I'm being cold, but Robert pisses me off. He's the one made us do all those laps and the six a.m. trash pickup in the first place.

A whistle blows and we both follow it. Coach is standing in the doorway to his office. "Let's get started!" he calls out.

Robert rocks himself up to his feet. This is the first time Robert and I have ever been alone anywhere. He's holding the list like it's covered with scum. I try to sound bored. "You want me to read it for you?"

His head snaps up. He glances over at T's office. "Up and back guard," he croaks.

It's a drill we usually do at practice. Coach is standing by the office door watching. I start dribbling and Robert puts a hand on my back. He reaches all around trying to knock the ball away. It takes me about three minutes to get the ball to the foul line and he knocks it away like ten times.

He seems to be getting into it, enjoying harassing me just like that first time we met doing this same drill back in tenth grade. He probably figures this is not going to be so bad after all. He gets to make me miserable for half an hour every day.

We do four different drills. Robert says the name of the drill and that's all he says. When the clock hits five, he just walks out. Doesn't say anything. Just turns his back and walks away. I don't want to be in the locker room alone with him so I shoot foul shots for another fifteen minutes till I'm pretty sure he's cleared out. A half an hour of just me and Robert is plenty for one day.

chapter seventeen
WHIRL

"How was your tutorial yesterday, gentlemen?"

T has us sitting on the bench after practice again the next day. Just me and Robert. We sit there staring at all the interesting things in the empty gym. We sure don't look at each other.

At first we don't say anything, but that makes me nervous with T so I say, "Fine."

T looks to Robert and Robert nods his head. "Okay. Run it the same way again today. Let's get started."

We start again without a word to each other. T goes into the locker room. Robert does his best to harass me. When he knocks it away, he stands there shaking his head and doing this fake chuckling stuff that annoys the heck out of me. And that's how it goes for the next two weeks. We don't even talk. Robert doesn't even say the name of the drill anymore. He sets up and I know right away what we're doing. We just keep doing it, the same thing, every day after practice.

The thing is, now that we're two weeks into it, I hate to admit it, but I'm handling the ball with more control and starting to get around Robert. The getting around Robert part I like. And I like that it bugs him.

Everything else on the court is cool. We are 7–0. Undefeated! We're in first place in the Colonial County League and people are beginning to pay attention. I'm still starting. On the court, things are great.

Thank God it's Friday, though. I won't have to do this for two days. In the last drill today, I whirl on Robert, go right past him and in for two. He takes the ball to set up again and mumbles, "Elbow me."

There was no elbow, or at least nothing illegal. I get sick when people complain about nothing on the court. This is typical Robert. "Oh, don't be a baby."

Robert won't look at me. "Elbow me again—"

I wipe the sweat off my face with my shirt. "Just play the game."

"You suck." He says it to the wall, but it pisses me off.

I walk over to get in front of him.

"Gentlemen."

It's Coach T. He's like twenty feet away and I never heard him coming. I can't believe such a big guy can move around so quietly. He tilts his head like he's real interested. "Robert, what is it about Raymond's dribbling that you feel specifically needs improvement?"

Robert's looking everywhere but at us.

"Robert?"

"Dunno," he mumbles.

Coach T talks all calm and smooth. "Robert, I've asked you to complete this task as a member of the team. I need you to be clear. Now, what is it Raymond does wrong in his ballhandling?"

Robert is ready to spit. He looks out at the bleachers as he talks. "He got no left."

The words sting. Even though I'm a lot better, I've got to improve my left hand, but I don't like to use it. It's so much weaker. It doesn't feel normal.

"That's good advice, Raymond. Work on your left hand. Try to use only your left for the rest of this session. And stay low."

"Okay, Coach."

T walks back into his office.

Robert waits until he's gone from sight, then in this little squeaky-girl voice, he says, "Okay, Coach. I kiss your butt, Coach."

"Shut up." Little jerk. I'd like to strangle him.

Robert tries to stare all bad at me. "Do somethin'." First time he looked at me today.

"How about I make you read a book? That might kill you."

"How about I go upside your head?" Robert cocks his head and takes a step toward me.

I put my left foot forward to lead with the left. "Oooh.

I'm scared. You're so bad." I'm not scared of Robert. I'd like to punch him.

He gives it up and goes into this mock disgust act, shaking his head to save face. "Come at me." He snaps the ball at me.

I catch it and dribble right at Robert. He angles his body and starts heading me toward the sideline. He's pressuring me to either switch hands or go out-of-bounds. I switch to my left and he slaps it away, chases it, picks it up, and lays it in.

"You got nuthin'," he calls back.

"Let's try it again." I grab the ball up. "C'mon, Robert. Get tough. D me up." I take the ball and square up in front of the basket. Close. So I won't have to dribble much. I start dribbling with my right hand. Robert starts to walk away. I drive right toward him, bump him hard, whirl on him, and score on a little hook layup.

"Not much of a stop there, Robert. Let's do it again."

He's stopped and looking now.

"C'mon. Try and stop me. I can score on you all day long." I get the ball and dribble right for him again. He Ds up with his hand on my hip. He pushes me hard as I make my move. I slap his hand away and give him a good elbow in the chest. The baby grabs my arm and pulls and the ball flies out-of-bounds. He grabs my arm!

I give him a good hard push in the chest that moves him off his feet. He bounces right back and jumps up and swings at me. The little jerk is throwing punches! I tie up his arms, but he's fast and he's swinging with both hands. We tangle up and hit the floor hard together.

"Hey!" The voice booms through the gym. It's like a drum. Coach T is standing by his office door. Most coaches would be running, pulling you apart. He just stands there. "Get up!"

We both straighten up and stand.

"Is that on the schedule?"

We just stand there breathing hard.

"Then, knock it off. Robert, what are you supposed to be doing right now? It's four fifty."

"He—"

"What—is—on—the—schedule?"

There's a long pause. All you can hear is our breathing coming fast and deep.

Robert mumbles, "Whirl."

"I can't hear you."

Robert says it louder, defiant-like, "*Whirl.*"

"Then do it."

He looks at me, then at T. "Man, he . . ."

More breathing. T is just standing there. Robert looks at the floor. He doesn't finish.

"Yes?" Coach is still way back by his office. Robert stands there, staring at the floor. T finishes up in a real level voice. "The schedule. Don't deviate."

Finally Robert turns away and says, "Yeah."

"Raymond?"

"Yeah, Coach?"

"Do the drills. And hold your tongues—both of you. All I want to hear is the ball bouncing. Understood?"

"No. I mean, okay."

Robert says nothing.

We start the drill.

chapter eighteen
BIG GULP

After tutorial I'm boiling. Robert almost bought it today. I run all the way home just to blow off some steam. When I finish my homework, I'm reading *Sports Illustrated* in my room and there's a knock at the door. I get it and there's Walter. "Hey, big boy, come on in."

He's wearing a big pair of overalls and an old gray jacket. He looks a little preoccupied, kind of looking around and not smiling. "Thanks, man. What's going on?"

"Nothing. You're not working tonight?"

"Nah. I took off."

I don't like the vibe I'm picking up. "Who's doing the egg stand?"

He looks at the ceiling. "I don't know. Nobody." He sounds totally disinterested. This is very weird. I know his father doesn't take him missing work real well.

"You wanna hang out here?"

"Yeah, I guess."

"What's Stella up to?" Usually on a night off, Walter

would be hanging with Stella. I hadn't seen Walter at night in a while. Friday nights with *Dr. Shock* seems like a long time ago.

"I don't know."

We walk into the living room. My father looks up. He's in his chair, my mother is in hers. They're watching TV. "Walter! *Jak sic pan*?" Which means "How are you?" in Polish. My father likes to talk Polish to Walter, because he knows some.

Walter answers in Polish, "*Dobrze.*" Which means "fine."

"Good. Good."

My mom says, "How's your mother, Walter?"

"Oh, she's good. She said to say hi."

My mom sighs. "I remember when your mother and I were in school at OLC. We went all the way through twelfth grade together. From kindergarten! Did you know that?"

Walter seems distracted. "Yeah," is all he offers.

My mother sees Walter is not in a talkative mood. She shrugs. "Well, it was a long time ago. I have to call her."

Walter says, "Hmmm."

I put an arm on Walter. "Yeah, let's get something in the kitchen."

Walter follows me in and plops heavily into a chair at the table. His work boots are untied. I put out a couple of plates and glasses.

"So, Stella's away?"

Walter looks all disgusted. "She broke up with me."

I don't know what to say. I just get some cold chicken out of the fridge and a couple of root beers. "You want a root beer?"

He waves his hand at me. "Yeah. Fine. Whatever."

I sit down and we start gnawing on the chicken. Finally I say something. "That sucks. What happened?"

"I don't know. She calls and tells me this out of the blue."

"Girls are something else, man." I think about Stacey. I swig some root beer.

"Yeah. She's telling me all about how I got problems, right? I do this. I do that. Like she's perfect?" He waves his hand, dismissing the whole thing. "Aw, who cares?"

I gnaw on a drumstick. We both chew for quite a while. Then I figure I should pick up the ball. "Hey. You still got your friends, right?"

Walter nods, his face low over the plate. "Exactly."

I want to lighten this up. There's nothing sadder than Walter looking down. "You still got kielbasa."

A little grin starts. Then he chimes in, "Still got hoagies."

"Yep. Still got cheese popcorn."

"Still got toilet paper."

I choke on my chicken, laughing. "What?"

Walter laughs too. "My dad said when things were tough when they were little, they didn't have toilet paper. They had to use newspaper."

"*Yeeccch.* I'm eating here!" I throw some chicken skin on him. He yells, leans over, and thumps me and I thump him back and pretty soon we're banging around the kitchen whacking each other as hard as we can.

"Oww. Owww!" I'm in pain, but laughing at the same time.

My father yells in. "What are you doing in there!?"

Walter giggles and calls back, "It's okay, Mr. W. I'm just murdering Raymond."

My father calls back, "Well, do it more quietly. I'm trying to watch something here."

Walter jumps on my back and we fall to the floor with a huge crash, and I am crying now from laughing.

My father yells again, "Walter! Raymond! If you break anything in there I'll kick both your cans!"

We chorus back, "Yes sir!" Then we fall apart again.

After we stop laughing and wipe all the tears away, Walter looks a lot better. He's got his grin going again. We talk some more and conclude that girls are some sort of communist plot or something. Particularly Polish girls. He finally leaves at about eleven. On the way out the door he claps me on the back.

"You still de man, Ray," he says. "Thanks."

Friday night is excellent for me! Fifteen points, eight rebounds. We win by ten and our record is 11–0. Still undefeated! On Saturday at practice Robert and I accidentally run into each other on a play, and he bounces off me on his toes with his hands up like he's ready to fight. I'm wondering if he's going to try to do anything again, but there's nothing. He tries to act so cool. He hardly talks to anybody on the team. He's too great for all of us.

Fortunately, I don't have to do tutorial on Saturday. It's a day off from Robert. After practice I'm in the hall waiting for Winnie, and a couple of cheerleaders walk by carrying a table. Then out of the auditorium comes Stacey straining to carry a table by herself!

I hustle over. "Here, let me give you a hand." I grab one end and she lets go so I get the rest of it, flip it over and set up the legs. "There you go."

"Thanks, Ray! You are so sweet."

And you are so good-looking. That's what I'd like to say. I settle for, "No problem. What's this all about?" I try to keep my voice steady.

She gets some papers and rolls of red tickets out of a cardboard box and puts them on the table along with some pens and a cash box. "We're raising money for Children's Hospital. There's a play here in the auditorium later and we're going to be selling raffle tickets to people as they leave. Do you want to buy any?"

This other cheerleader calls over from down the hall, "Stacey, where do we write the numbers?"

Stacey hops up. "Excuse me a second. I'm coordinator."

"Yeah?"

"Sure. President of the student volunteers at Children's Hospital. That's me." She laughs and curtsies. "Stay right there." I try not to stare at her rear as she walks away, but I fail pretty miserably. She talks to the girl, then jogs back and says, "So? Are you interested?"

Lots of ways to answer that question, but I'm going to play it safe. "Yeah. How much are they?"

She leans over the table to me. "A dollar."

I reach in my wallet. I know there's a five. And I know I'm not going to see any more money till next Friday. "I'll take five. Man, you're involved in a lot of stuff."

She smiles. "Not really." She flips her hair around. "It's for a real good cause, anyway. You should see these kids. We were over there last week, reading to them. They're so cute. We're going to use the money to buy books for each kid."

"You know I do English tutoring over at the OLC center twice a month. I work with one guy. And he's really picking it up. I really like it. I'm thinking about teaching."

She widens her eyes. "I didn't know that. That's great."

She rips the tickets off the roll, writes some stuff down, and says, "Here. Write your phone number on these and keep this part. The drawing is later today. You'll be notified if you've won."

Something witty comes to me! "Well, I guess that's one way you can get my phone number."

She laughs! I made Stacey laugh! "Very cute," she says.

I shrug. "That's what my mom says too." I am goofing around with Stacey!

She tilts her head and raises an eyebrow. "You know. You're really playing well. I'm like proud of you."

Oh, man! This girl actually likes me. I know it! "Thanks. So are—I mean—"

The same girl calls over, "Sta-cey! Where do these go?"

She shrugs. "Sorry. I'll see you, okay?"

"Right. Bye."

I fill in my phone number, take one last look, and walk down the hall. She is so cool. She's nice. She's smart. Those wind pants fit like—man!

Winnie is leaning against the wall grinning at me. When I get close he says, "C'mon now, lover boy."

I lean into him and whisper, "Man, did you see her smile at me?"

"Yeah. It was cosmic. C'mon, you wanna shoot a little?"

We walk out. "I'm serious. I think this girl likes me."

Winnie laughs. "Did I see you give her money?"

I pause. "Yeah. It's for a good cause."

He laughs louder. "You give me money, I be nice to you too."

I laugh, but give him a shot in the arm. "Shut up, man. You don't know nothing about it."

He keeps laughing. "I'm sure I don't."

We go over to the outdoor courts behind the school. It's a pretty warm day for December so we take off our coats, keep our sweats on, and run some heavy one-on-one so that we're actually sweating. Winnie and I both have this thing in common, where we will play ball constantly. After a two-hour practice, we're ready to go play again. We love it that much.

I got the height on him, but he's got the speed on me, so it works out to be pretty even. I'm pumped, though, because of Stacey. I just wish she wasn't going out with Brock. We play to twenty-one three times and then start warming down, just shooting.

"How's things with you and your tutor?" he says, laughing.

"What do you think?"

"Not good, huh?"

"I can't stand him. He can't stand me." I shoot a corner that is way off.

Winnie grabs it and banks it in. "You're handling the ball better."

I just look at him and he cracks up. "It's true." He laughs.

I shake my head, but have to laugh too. "There's got to be a better way to learn than with that punk."

He passes to me. "Hey, Robert ain't so bad. He's stuck-up and a pain in the butt, but there's worse people than Robert."

I shoot. "Yeah, like Rudy."

Winnie grabs the rebound and passes it back. "Or that Walter boy you hang with."

"You know Walter?"

He snorts. "Yeah. He's that big redneck boy."

I feel embarrassed. Like ashamed I know Walter. "Ah, he just says a lot of stuff. He doesn't do anything." I take a jumper.

"Yeah, that's probably what Hitler's friends used to say. 'Oh, don't worry about that stuff old Adolf's talkin'. He ain't serious. He's just bein' stupid.'"

I force a laugh, but I don't say anything else about it. We put our coats back on. Winnie says, "You wanna hit 7-Eleven?"

I check my pockets, but I just spent all my money on raffle tickets. "No. I'm tapped out."

"It's on me."

We walk over. Winnie buys a Big Gulp for nighty-nine cents. It's lemon-lime, which is my favorite. We sit down on the sidewalk and lean against the bricks on the side of the building. As long as you stay in the sun it's warm enough to hang outside. Winnie takes a hit and then passes the cup to me.

I wave it away. "No, that's okay, man."

"Here. Have some. I can't drink this whole thing."

I'm holding the soda in my hand and I think, he drank from it and now I'm going to. If it had been Ziggy or Pruze or Walter, I wouldn't have had a thought about it. But, it was Winnie. Black lips had been on the cup. I embarrassed myself again. That I even thought about it. I take a nice long drink and pass it back.

I have to say something. Make sure he didn't notice anything. "That hits the spot."

"You know it."

There's no way I can picture Walter doing the same thing. And I gotta wonder—does that matter?

chapter nineteen

SARAH

Urban Politics starts today. First day of second semester. It's an elective. I'm able to take just about all electives now. All my applications are in. All four schools have good teacher ed. programs, but I really want State. I'd love to be a teacher as good as Paterson. The main thing is—I'm going to college. That'll be a first in my family.

Winnie's in Urban Politics, too. Paterson's teaching it in his regular room so we sit in our old seats, Winnie right in front of me. Mr. Paterson says, "We're going to begin working together in dyads to do some research and presentation preparation. I'll assign you a topic."

I'm hoping Winnie and I are going to be partners. That's what dyads are. If you've had Paterson you get used to his terminology. I get the topic "Frank Hague: Urban Mayor." Paterson knows I'm into this stuff and that my mother's father used to live in Jersey City where Hague was mayor, so I'm not surprised by my topic. I am surprised by my partner, however—Sarah Whitney.

Sarah always sits in the front row. Every class. She hangs with these two other girls, Margaret Brennan and Andrea Litowitz. I'm okay in history and English, but they're geniuses in everything.

Sarah and I move our chairs so we face each other except she's looking at her books and not at me. She doesn't look like she's going to say anything, so I start things up. This could be a long class. "Okay, so Frank Hague, huh?"

"Yes," she says. You can hardly hear her.

She's still not looking at me. She's arranging her notebook. She's got on a white blouse and a gray skirt. And a pin on her shirt. A silver musical note. She looks like a librarian. We've got to get through this, so I keep talking. "Some of my family is originally from Jersey City. That's where Frank Hague was mayor."

"Really?" She's glances up. I can see she's surprised.

"Yep. They called him Frank 'I am the law' Hague. He was sort of a dictator, but he looked out for people. You had a problem, like you needed a job, you went down to city hall and he helped you out." I like talking about Hague. It's something I know about almost firsthand and I think it's interesting.

Sarah interjects, "If you promised to vote for him."

"Yeah. Something like that. My grandparents loved him. All my relatives did." I can see her face changing expression as she considers stuff. It's a little round, but not fat or anything.

She's back to looking at her books, but she says, "A benevolent dictator. As long as you go along, you get along, to an extent."

I think about that. "Yeah. Good way to say it." As we talk about outlines and topics and all, I notice she is actually okay-looking. If you don't mind somebody a little bit rounded.

Practice goes fine and then Robert and I meet for the dreaded daily tutorial. I hope Coach ends this thing soon. I'm wondering if we're going to mix it up again, but I don't think so.

Today he says nothing from start to finish. He goes in and I stick around and do my foul shots. It's funny, as long as Robert keeps his mouth shut I can handle it. I like that I'm getting better at it. I like that I'm getting around him some, but he's still a jerk.

And the team is doing really good. We've won five in a row. We're 15–1, with the one loss to Clayton Academy. They're a local prep school. They've got players who are PGs, post-graduates. Guys that should be in college already. It wasn't a league game either, so nobody flipped out over losing that one. It's like it didn't count.

I'm still starting at forward. I get out there and it's like it was meant to be. I belong out there. I get on the court and I stop thinking, get my invisible helmet on, and just play.

When I'm done shooting fouls I go in the locker room and Pruze is still there, sitting on a bench putting powder on his feet. I rap him on the head with my knuckles. "What are you doin' here?"

"Just got out of the whirlpool. My feet are killing me. Everybody keeps stepping on 'em."

I sit down on the bench next to him. "Man, you got big, ugly feet. Looks like a grandma's feet."

"You're a real joker, Ray. These dogs hurt." Pruze puts his socks on real slow and careful. "Hey, man. What is wrong with your buddy, the Egg Man? Has he finally tripped out?"

I get my sneakers and socks off and try to change quick. I've got a lot of homework. "Ah, Walter's bummin'. He came over the other night and told me Stella broke up with him."

"Bummin'? Try 'psycho.' She dumped him because he's acting like a moron. I swear, Ray, he's looking for trouble. Did you hear what went down in his shop class today?" Pruze pulls on his big old jeans.

"No."

He lowers his voice a little. "Man, you don't hear anything. Walter mixed it up with Seven."

"Seven? Shoot!" Seven is the baddest guy in the school, black *or* white. He's this slick, thin, shaved-headed brother who always dresses like he's going to an event at the Hilton. He's also always beating up on somebody or shaking them down for money. I'm not even sure what grade he's in, but he is one bad dude.

Pruze leans in. "Yeah, and get this. They're saying Walter had a hunk of metal in his hand when he hit Seven. They *carried* Seven out. Walter's suspended. They would have expelled him if Mr. Kearney actually saw it happen."

Shit. My stomach drops, but I don't want Pruze to think I'm worried. I stay cool. "You know Walter. He does stupid stuff sometimes."

Pruze pops his eyes. "Ray? Hello? I just said he hit him with a chunk of metal! He could have *killed* the guy!"

I answer kind of quick and sharp. "All right. I hear you."

Pruze stands up and buttons his flannel shirt. "Look, I know you guys are boys from way back and all that, but I'm sorry, he's losing it."

"Okay. I'll talk to him."

"You better talk to him. That boy's got something loose."

I give him a little smile and hop up off the bench. Let him know it's all cool. "Yeah. Okay. No problem."

Pruze stands there. He is not smiling. "I'm serious, Ray. Watch yourself with him."

When I get home I try calling Walter's house, but it just rings and rings. I try five different times, then give it up. The next day at school he doesn't show up at the cafeteria. I go looking for him, but can't find him anywhere which makes sense if he's suspended, but then why isn't he answering the phone?

Urban Politics starts off with all of us listening to Paterson for about five minutes and then meeting with our partners. I'm actually looking forward to this. It was kind of interesting working with Sarah.

It goes just like yesterday only she talks more. She's easy to work with. A good listener and smart, too. Paterson did not give us a lot of time to do this so I ask her, "You want to get passes for the library? I've got study hall last period."

She clears her throat. "Well, we could do that, or we could meet at my house right after school."

I almost can't think of what to say. This is the shy genius girl, asking if we can meet at her *house*! Then I remember I'm still on the basketball team. "I have practice today. Could we do it later?"

"What time is practice over?"

"About five. Is five thirty okay?"

"Sure, we can work for an hour or so before dinner."

She gives me directions to her house, which I knew was going to be in Regent's Park. Regent's Park is where all the smart, rich kids live. I've been through there riding my bike, and sometimes when I was little on Halloween we would hit those big houses for big-time candy.

At lunch I don't mention it to Stoshy or Gerard. I don't think they'd be real impressed with me going over to Sarah Whitney's house. Instead I ask, "Do you guys know what happened with Walter?"

Stoshy opens up his lunch bag. "Suspended. For a week."

"That's what Pruze said. I mean, why did he flip out like that? Pruze said he hit Seven."

Gerard leans forward and whispers. "Yeah, but don't say

anything about it. Mr. Kearney never actually saw it and Walter denied it. All the black kids were sayin' yeah he did it, and all the rest of us were saying no he didn't, so Kearney gave it up and just suspended Walter for being too close to the action. He figures Walter did it, but he can't prove it."

"What the hell happened exactly?"

Gerard nods at Stoshy. "We're making these metal caps. Like for the top of a post. Walter and Seven were up at the lathe trying to get a turn. Seven gave him an elbow and said, 'Get out the way, white trash.' That was it. Walter turned around and clocked him with this chunk of steel he had in his hand. Boom! One move."

Stoshy nods and snaps his fingers. "It happened just like that."

I shake my head. "Man, that is screwed up. He actually hit him with a piece of metal?"

Gerard wrinkles his forehead. "It wasn't like he planned it. He just had it in his hand."

Stoshy says, "Yeah. It just happened. Besides it's not like Seven doesn't deserve a hit in the head."

"I've got to talk to Walter."

They both look at each other. Gerard talks to his sandwich. "Whatever. Good luck."

Then we all start eating and eventually we talk about other stuff, but there's no goofing.

During practice I keep thinking about where Walter is and how Stoshy and Gerard were okay with this shop thing.

Maybe it was just a reaction. Unavoidable. But, he hit him with a chunk of metal. Like a weapon.

I think about it all during tutorial and hardly notice Robert, which is saying something. After I finish up and get dressed I remember about Sarah. And I get a good feeling. I catch a ride over there with Pruze in his tank. Walter's in the back of my mind, but now Sarah's in the front.

"Who you going to see in Regent's Park?" He's drumming on the steering wheel.

"This girl I'm working on a project with."

"You social climber, you. Who is it?"

"Sarah Whitney. Drop me here, man."

He pulls over real hard and squeals the brakes. "Sarah Whitney, huh? Well, don't get into a game of Scrabble 'cause she'll dust your sorry behind. And remember you're a gentleman. Hang on to your Polish pickle or provide your own protection."

"Such priceless wisdom." I slap the door and he takes off honking the horn.

I look down into Regent's Park. It's all tall, dark trees and little lights lining the lawns. Sarah's street slopes down gradually, and winds like a trail in a real park. It smells deep and damp. The houses are set way back off the street.

Sarah's house is the fifth one in on the right. It's a big old white Colonial with a black metal eagle on the clapboard in the front. I go up a brick walkway and ring the bell and Sarah answers. She smiles and pushes her glasses up on her nose.

"Hi, Ray. Come in."

She used my name. That's the first time she's done that. "Thanks, Sarah." I figure I better use her name right back. There's something about using the other person's name.

You go in, you're standing on a stone floor. There are carpets on these real polished wood floors on each side of the stone. There's two fireplaces that I can see already and all old Colonial stuff everywhere. I'm looking at the house, but I'm checking Sarah out, too. She's got her hair pulled back. You can really see how round her face is, but it's cute, like a little moon.

"Did you have any trouble finding it?"

"No. Good directions."

"Would you like some hot chocolate?"

"Sure." I'm just standing in one place. This is very new territory.

"We can work in the dining room." I follow her to the left past a huge grandfather clock. "Have a seat. I'll be right back."

I watch her walk out. Her cords fit nice. I sit down at a big dark table. She's already got stuff laid out ready to go. Paper, pencils, sharpener. The room is huge. Two of our dining rooms could fit in here.

She comes back with a couple of mugs of hot chocolate and a plate of chocolate chip cookies. "So . . ." She puts the plate in front of me. ". . . Frank Hague. Benevolent Dictator."

We write and talk about Hague, politics, cities, corruption, our outline, who does what, and the hour is over just like that. Then out of the blue she switches gears. "How was your practice?"

"Good."

"You like basketball a lot, I guess."

I'm so surprised I just blurt, "I love it."

"Really?"

I guess "love" sounds kind of strong. "Yeah. I'd rather play ball more than anything."

She gives a little laugh. "Well, that's something."

She's putting her things away so I pack up. I'd like to keep her talking. "How about you? What are you into?"

She looks down and shakes her head. "Oh, reading. Violin. Writing."

"Writing? Like what?"

She hesitates, then walks toward the door. I follow her with my stuff. "Poetry."

I start to ramble. "No kidding. I could never write poetry. I can write reports and stuff, and maybe a story, but poetry—out of the question. Why poetry?"

She looks back at me and hesitates for a second. "You can say things with poetry you can't say any other way."

I never read poetry except when I have to in class and it never does a lot for me. Probably basketball doesn't do a lot for many poets, either. "I'd like to see some of your poetry sometime."

She smiles and shakes her head. "It's not very good. I don't think you'd be impressed."

"I'd like to see it anyway."

She opens the door and says, "Well, I've got to help get dinner on the table."

"Right." I step outside. It's already dark and getting cold.

"Do you need a ride home or anything?"

"No. I'm walking. I walk a lot." Which is very true, since I have no car.

"Okay. Bye. I'll see you in school."

"Thanks, Sarah. Bye." Used the name.

She smiles again and pushes her glasses up. "Bye, Ray."

chapter twenty
MY HEART LIKE THE SKY

After dinner I try calling Walter, but the phone just keeps ringing again. If he's suspended and at home, he should be answering the phone. If he's not he should be at school. Something's up.

I borrow the van and drive out to the farm. It's mostly fields with a little white house in the middle and two long white chicken houses about a hundred yards behind it. I've only been here twice before. Walter's never been keen on us hanging around his house.

There are no outside lights on, so I leave my headlights on and the engine running. I walk up the peeling wooden steps to the front door and knock.

No answer. I knock again and wait. I can hear a TV inside. I knock one more time and Walter's father appears. He stares down at me through the screen. His face is stubbly, his eyes are red. He looks annoyed. "What?"

I try to manage a smile. "Hi, Mr. Wasko. Is Walter around?"

He wipes his nose with the back of his hand. "No."

He doesn't say anything else. Just stares at me. I take a step back down the stairs. "Okay. Could you tell him I stopped by then?"

I stand there waiting for him to say okay or something. He just keeps staring. Like he can't believe what he's seeing. Then finally he says, "I hear yer a nigger lover."

My body stiffens. What do you say to that! I take the rest of the stairs at a trot and get in the car and reverse out as fast as I can. He stands at the door watching me all the way to the road.

In the morning Paterson gives us more class time to prepare our reports. Sarah starts talking about Frank Hague, but I stop listening. Her face is interesting. Very smooth. And she has dark brown eyes. Deep. Like a thinker, which she obviously is. I'm comparing her to other girls I know. Like Stella or Theresa Micinski or Jeanine Pieslak. They're all nice. They're okay-looking too. Sarah's different, though. I get the feeling there's a lot going on under the surface.

Then I think of Stacey. Stacey is, I don't know, like out of a movie. Sometimes I think I can ask Stacey out, but then I think again, do I even qualify? And what about Brock? I think I'm just being delusional about Stacey and me anyway. And now here's Sarah.

Suddenly Paterson interrupts my daydream. "Okay, people. Let's pack it up."

Sarah starts putting her stuff away and says, "So, tomorrow for the oral report, you'll do the opening?"

"Yeah, and you do 'Part One: His Early Life,' I'll do 'Part Two: His Years as Mayor,' and you close, right? Five minutes on each section."

"That sounds good." She snaps her binder shut.

I try to think of something else to say, but all I can come up with is, "Yep."

She's standing there, fidgeting around with her things. Then she opens her history book and pulls out a folded piece of typing paper. "Here." She hands me the paper.

"Is this for the report?"

She looks a little tense all of a sudden. "No. You—well, you said you wanted to see one."

I'm thinking what is she nervous about, and then I remember—the poetry! I smile real big. "Oh. Yeah. Definitely. Thanks!"

"Read it later, okay?"

"Absolutely."

She smiles and turns, leaving the room with her two smart girlfriends. I fold the paper up and put it in my shirt pocket. Then I think about it, and put it in my rear pants pocket. Things are generally safer there as long as I remember to get them out before they end up in the wash.

Winnie comes over as I'm packing up my books. He nods toward Sarah leaving. "You're getting along all right."

"Yeah. She's okay."

"Yeah? I thought you were all hot on Stacey."

We walk out into the hall. "Yeah, well—I don't know."

He laughs. "I'm goofin', man. Stacey's a goddess. What are you gonna do?"

"Yeah." I shake my head. He's right. She is a goddess. I'm never going to ask her out. "Are you hanging out with Bernadette?"

He widens his eyes and gives me this fake annoyed look. "I can't tell you about my private life. You be writin' it down and sellin' it to the *National Enquirer.*"

"Yeah. They would be real interested."

"Hey, I'll catch you at practice."

"Later."

Winnie splits off. I head into the lunchroom and there sitting alone at our table is Walter. I hustle over, give him a slap on the back, and slide into the chair next to him.

"Walter! Where you been? I've been calling you. I stopped out to see you."

"Yeah. I heard. Thanks." He claps me on the shoulder. "I've been over at Teddy's house relaxing. I get tense with all this schoolwork." He jerks his body all around like he's having a convulsion.

"Why isn't anybody answering your phone?"

He rolls his eyes. "My old man ripped it out of the wall. Two telemarketers called during dinner the other night. So that's his solution." He shakes his head. "That'll last for a few days."

I think about his dad all drunk and mean. "Good to see you, man."

"Yeah, you too."

"Anything new with Stella?"

"Nah. I hear she's going out with this creep from OLC now. Ah, it don't matter."

I lean my chair back against the wall behind us and Walter joins me. I lower my voice. "So you got suspended, huh?"

"Yeah. They're always picking on me around here. You know that. I got a week this time. I'm hanging here to see Teddy about something."

"I heard you laid Seven out with a piece of metal. You have to cool out, man."

He bounces up off the wall. He's not smiling now. "Who told you that?" He gets louder. "It was some punk from the basketball team, right?"

I straighten up. "Cool out, man. Take it easy."

He stands up. "I'm serious, Ray."

I stay in my seat. "I'm just seein' if you're okay." I hold my ground.

"Who you gonna believe, Ray? Someone you grew up with or some black boy from Jefferson Park?" He balls his hands up into fists.

"Believe what? You didn't hit him?"

For an answer Walter grabs the edge of the table with both hands and flips it over. I jump out of the way. Slam! Food, books, and papers scatter across the floor.

The whole cafeteria goes silent. Then cheers break out. A woman teacher I don't know comes running over. "Hey. Wait! Come back here!" But Walter is hauling butt out the door. I watch his big coat disappear into the crowd in the hall.

I help her pick the table up. "Who was that boy?" she asks, looking out at the hall.

I follow her gaze. "I'm not sure."

At night I lie in bed thinking about Walter. He's getting crazy. Even for Walter. And I'm feeling like I'm a big part of why. But what can I do? Maybe the suspension will cool him out. I hope. One thing's for sure, my life compartment plan stinks.

I take off my pants and check my pockets before they go in the laundry. Then I feel Sarah's poem in my back pocket! I've got to read this thing. I unfold it. I didn't want to touch it in school, where someone might see.

It's typed. That figures. It's a haiku poem, with the five-seven-five syllables in the three lines. We learned how to write these back in seventh grade. I read it slowly, taking my time to try to hear it.

> *My heart, like the sky*
> *lilting, high, light, loving, full,*
> *would you hold it close?*

I read it two more times. I always thought haiku had to be about crickets or frogs and nature stuff. I'm not completely sure, but I'm reading this as a heavy-duty love poem. I mean what else could it be? I think this girl wrote me a love poem! And I like it!

chapter twenty-one
FIVE SPADES

I get lucky and find Sarah first thing in the morning in the hall. Actually I stand around her locker for five minutes reading the same two posters about the school musical and safety regulations over and over till she shows up. So it's not exactly all luck.

She comes out of the stairwell and spots me. I see a smile. I say hey and try to find a way to lean on the wall, but there's a fire extinguisher and a door next to her locker so I just stand.

"Hi. How are you?" She's wearing a big knit cardigan and she's holding a violin case.

"I'm good. Ready for the presentation?" I ask.

Real confident she says, "I should think so."

I have to laugh. "Good. Good."

She lifts her chin. "Do *you* have everything?"

"Oh, yeah, of course. What am I? A slacker?"

She giggles.

I don't really want to talk about the presentation, and we don't have a lot of time before class. Unfortunately, I'm not real smooth at shifting gears subtly in conversation so I just do it.

"I read your poem last night."

The color goes up from her neck right into her cheeks. She's instantly red. "Oh, I shouldn't have written that. I mean, it was just—"

"No. It was good. I liked it. I—it—you know—"

We both bust out laughing. Sarah giggles again. "We better be more articulate than this during our presentation."

"Yeah. That's for sure."

The laughter fades into a couple of chuckles. I should ask. I'm going to ask. I ask. "Uh, Sarah. I have a game tonight. Would you want to come watch?" This is almost like asking her out. Pretty darn close, anyway.

She scrunches her face up. "Oh, Ray. I'd like to, but I have a concert tonight. I'm playing in the County Youth Orchestra."

I shrug. "Oh, well. No biggie."

"No. Next time. I really do want to see you play."

"That would be great. Only a couple of games left, though."

The bell rings. "I've got to go get a folder. I'll see you in class." She waves and starts walking backwards.

I do the backwards walk too. "Right. See you."

She's cute. And real interesting. I still can't believe she wrote that poem.

As I walk over to school that night for the game, I think about our presentation today. It went real well. Very smooth.

The class applauded. Paterson said, "Excellent work. Very clear. Lots of good information. Two people who worked very well together." Sarah turned around in her seat and gave me a wink. I gave her a thumbs-up. Then she mouthed the words, "I love you!" in a real exaggerated way before she turned back around. She's definitely keeping me thinking about her!

The other thing I'm thinking about is our team. We are 16–2. Pruze was right. We're having a great season. In fact, we're heading for the league championship. Only one other team has a record like ours and that's Yorkville.

Pruze has been like a wild man in the middle. I love playing up front with Al. We pick for each other all night and it's like we've got the sixth sense going. He knows where I'm going to be and I know what he's going to do. We got the three great shooting guards rotating in—Winnie, Ziggy, and of course, Robert.

The incredible thing with Robert, though, is that it's like T has gotten him under control. For the first time since I've known Robert, he isn't throwing up junk. If he does, T sits him instantly and talks to him. Robert is also leading the league in scoring. What can I say? He's good. A jerk. But good.

This is our second-to-last game. It's Fairview. We beat them by twelve last time so it should be no problem and sure enough the game turns out to be a walk. Come third quarter, we're leading by fourteen and getting stronger. We're doing whatever we want on the court and T is doing a lot of substitutions, so everybody can get some serious playing time.

They're shooting a foul and T calls for a sub. Al goes in for Pruze and then I see Larry coming in and he's tapping me. Me and Pruze both go out and sit.

Larry and Al give each other a bump and line up for the foul shot. I'm wiping sweat off my face with a towel. That's when I hear it. "Five Spades! Hey, Five Spades!" It's definitely Rudy yelling from up in the stands behind our bench. I'd recognize his screechy voice anywhere. He starts chanting it and pumping his arms. "Five Spades! Five Spades! Five Spades!" He's pointing at the court.

Five Spades? What is that about? Like in cards? I look back at him and then down at the court. I see what he's screaming about. There's five black guys from our team on the court.

The real dopey thing is that some of the other guys in the crowd start chanting it with him and clapping their hands. "Five Spades! Five Spades!" Then one of the guys starts making like a disco "whoop, whoop" noise in between the "Five Spades!" so it's "Five Spades! Whoop! Whoop! Five Spades! Whoop! Whoop!"

It's totally stupid, but Rudy's little crowd is getting into it. Once play starts again, they stop. But on the next foul shot they start again. I glance back. Rudy is standing and pumping his skinny arms and rocking and swaying back and forth.

"Five Spades! Five Spades!"

Coach T calls to me down the bench, "Raymond. Back in for Larry." I get up and go over to the scorer's table and check in. The horn blows and I head onto the court, slapping hands with Larry.

"Booooo! Booooo! Five Spades! We want Five Spades! We want Five Spades!" Rudy and his pals are on their feet, cupping their hands around their mouths. I quick look back at the shooter like I didn't even notice, but it bugs me.

A few minutes later, the horn blows. Pruze checks in and they boo him, too. He blows kisses back at them. Coach yells, "Stanley! Focus!"

Pruze nods and lines up on the lane for the foul shot. He wiggles his butt though and grabs his shorts and almost moons them. He's cracking up. I wish I could stay as cool as Pruze.

We finally win it by ten. Al, Pruze, and I all had twelve points each. Winnie had fourteen. Robert had sixteen. Balanced scoring! T will be happy. He loves balanced scoring. The only thing that spoils it is the "Five Spades" garbage. What if a bunch of us from Greenville started cheering for five white guys on the court? I'm sure that would go over real well.

On the way out of the locker room, Winnie and I stop in the hall to wait for Pruze and some of the other guys. We're going to have a pizza at Caputo's. I'm looking around the hall to see if any of the "Five Spades" jerks are out here. I'm feeling pretty pissed about it, especially the booing.

Winnie comes out into the hall with a copy of the stat sheet in his hand. "Look at this. You got *ten* rebounds! Ball must be taking some funny bounces if you can do that."

"Yeah, I know. Hey, did you hear that Five Spades crap?"

He doesn't look up. He's still reading the sheet. "What, am I deaf?"

"Yeah, well, what do you think?"

Winnie frowns. "What do you mean, what do I think?"

"I don't know. I figured you guys might say something."

"Who guys? Say like what?" I just look at him. He wrinkles his face up. "Get real, Ray. It's crap. It don't bear saying nuthin'." Then real suddenly, he pokes me in the ribs, looks down at the sheet again, and whispers, "Whup! Ten o'clock. Stacey heading this way."

I do a casual glance over. Stacey is walking in our direction with Brock on her arm. She's smiling and talking to him. He's huge. They just about get even with us, and Stacey shoots me a quick look. Those green eyes. And then she gives me a little wave. With Brock right on her arm, she waves to me! I'm just gaping. Winnie is, too.

"Mmmm," says Winnie finally.

I watch her walk away, with that little cheerleader skirt moving back and forth. Brock has his hand in the middle of her back and guides her out the door to the parking lot.

Whack! Something smacks me in the butt. Hard! I wheel around and Pruze is standing there grinning with his chemistry book in his hand.

"Hey! What are you staring at?" He wags a finger at me. "Remember, Big Brother is watching!"

I throw some fake punches at him while Winnie falls on the floor cracking up. Then we head out for pizza. Winnie leads the way doing his Stacey imitation, shaking his booty. Now Pruze is falling down laughing. Winnie is pretty funny. Actually, the both of them crack me up. I almost forget all about the Five Spades junk. But not completely.

chapter twenty-two
BIG HERO

The next three days flash by like commercials. All week I'm looking at Thursday. Thursday we play Yorkville. It's one of those real simple situations. If we win, we're Colonial County League champs. If we don't—they are. Simple. And scary.

This is the first morning Walter is officially supposed to be back in school. When I come into the cafeteria he's there spinning an empty Coke can around in little circles. He doesn't look at me when I sit down. I try to act regular. "What's up?"

"Hey."

"Anything goin' on?"

He keeps spinning his can. "Nope."

Then he stops and looks at me. All of a sudden I don't have anything to say. I don't want to talk about basketball, but it's the only thing on my mind. "Big game tonight."

As soon as it comes out, I want to take it back.

Walter returns to spinning the can. "Yeah. I heard."

I can't stop thinking about the game. I'm nervous, but on

the other hand, sometimes I can't wait to play and tear them up. This is a huge game. It's like school history. Franklin hasn't won a league title in ten years.

The bell rings. I get up. Walter doesn't move. "You coming?"

Walter watches his spinning can. "Nope."

I gather up my stuff. "Later then."

Walter looks at me. Studying me deep. "Yeah," is all he says.

When I see Sarah in class we exchange hi's, but now that our project's done, we're not having as many opportunities to talk. I would have to be real deliberate and walk her out of class, but she walks with the genius girls, so I'm not sure what my next move should be. I smile at her every chance I get, though. I don't want to lose the connection, but I don't want her to think I'm a grinning idiot, either, so finally I figure I should ask her to see the game.

At the end of Paterson's class I stop at her desk. "Hey, Sarah."

She looks up through the wire rims. "Hi, Ray."

"What would you think about going to the game tonight? Maybe doing something after?"

She gives me this pained look. "Oh. You're not going to believe this. We're going away for a long weekend to Boston. I'm leaving right after school today. I'm sorry."

"No. No. That's all right. Maybe another time."

She smiles. It's a cute little smile. Just the corners turning up. "That would be nice. I do want to, there's just so much going on right now."

I try to stay upbeat. "I know. No problem. I'll see you." It's probably better that she doesn't see the game anyway. It gives me one less thing to be nervous about.

If we win this game and get the title, we automatically go to the state tournament. We beat Yorkville twice this season, but not by a lot. And sometimes you don't want to play a team a third time because they've figured out a lot about how to play you by then. Everyone knows it could be another close one.

And that's exactly the way it ends up. It's the biggest home crowd of the year easy. Both teams are shooting well and everybody's hustling and playing defense. It's real good basketball. The whole game we go back and forth, trading the lead. We're up one, they're up one. We're up two, they go up two. Sometimes it's so intense I don't even know the score, just what I'm doing right at that moment.

T calls time-out and we sit down. I look at the clock. Thirty seconds! We're up one point. T—the voice of reason. "We have the lead. We have the ball. We have the advantage, right? They're going to press. This is their last chance. Use the diamond inbounds. Robert. Winnie. I want you both to come back for the ball. Everyone else head up court and draw your men with you. Stanley, you inbound. Ready?"

We all put a hand in and shout, "Let's go!"

We set up. The ref gives Pruze the ball and blows the

whistle, but on the inbounds Robert and Winnie can't break free. The clock is ticking.

I have to run back past half-court to give Pruze somebody to throw to. My guy didn't expect it so he's a step behind. Pruze throws it to me on the right side about fifteen feet behind the half line. I look for Robert but he's still covered. Robert can break the press. He can dribble through anything. If I could just get him the ball.

My man lays his sweaty chest right on me. I see a glimpse of Winnie, but he's got a guy fronting him. My guy is waving his hands all over me. He's like me on defense.

Robert gets loose for a second but there's too many hands. No one's open. My five seconds are going to be up. I have to put it on the floor. I have to dribble against the press.

I start dribbling.

Everybody sprints up court to clear out and draw their guys off so I can't be double-teamed. My guy starts pressing me into the sideline. He's got one hand on my back helping me get there. People are screaming my name.

Left hand. Left hand. Gotta go left hand. I switch over. Left. Switch it back. Right. Switch it back again, and put my body against him and whirl it, and all of a sudden, daylight. I'm ahead of him and sprinting down the middle of the court, dribbling with my left hand. I feel like I'm riding a bike with no hands, not exactly in control. I want to dish, but nobody will come off their man for me to dish to. They're waiting on me to drive to the hoop. I have to. I don't want to, but I have to.

I hit the lane, then explode up off the dribble. Two guys collapse in on me at the last second, but it's too late. I lay it up. Everybody goes up for the rebound. The ball bounces around the rim like a pinball in slow motion. Bang. Bim. Bang. And finally down and in.

Ugly, but in.

They try to inbound quick and get it back up court, but the buzzer sounds and they have to throw up this half-court desperation shot. Pruze catches it and throws it to the ceiling. *We're league champs!*

Kids are running all over the court. Pruze grabs me and picks me up. Winnie jumps on him. Then Al jumps in and I don't know who else because we all crash on the floor, rolling around on each other and yelling. The pep band is blaring and people are clapping and screaming. It's crazy.

After T lets us run around slapping hands with each other and the Yorkville guys, he motions us to follow him into the locker room. We go in bouncing and yelling. He still makes himself heard in the crowd and somehow he does it without raising his voice. "Great job, gentlemen. You have a lot to be proud of."

Everybody gets still and listens up. Al wipes away some tears.

"You played them right down to the wire. You kept your heads. You looked like champs. No practice tomorrow."

There's a huge cheer for that. Then T says, "Robert, Raymond, come over here." We eye each other. Everybody's yelling again. I have to bend over and put my hands on my knees to hear. "Congratulations, gentlemen."

We both nod. The guys are chanting, "We're Number One! We're Number One!" Why does T want to give us personal congratulations?

T ignores the noise. He touches Robert lightly on the shoulder. "Robert. We saw the result of your work here tonight. And I don't just mean your scoring or good defense. There is no way Raymond could have gone to the basket at the end like that without the tutorial you led."

Robert looks at him like, what is this? I'm feeling so good and high I can even lay a compliment on Robert. "Yeah, Robert. Thanks, man."

Robert doesn't change his expression. He grunts, "Whatever." And turns away.

T doesn't say anything else, he just gives me a nod and a clap on the back and goes into his office. Leave it to big-headed Robert to spoil the moment. He can kiss my rear. I jump into the craziness, yelling and screaming. After the game, Pruze goes to some drug-infested party no doubt. Me, Winnie, D-Man, and Ziggy go to Caputo's to celebrate.

On Friday at school I'm sitting in the cafeteria in the morning, and the quarterback from the football team, Ryan Ford, comes up to me, slaps me on the back, and says, "Ray. Way to go."

A minute later two teachers, Mr. Emmons and Ms.

Bartoletti, walk by. "Good job, Ray," Mr. Emmons says. Ms. Bartoletti smiles. "That was quite a shot you put in!"

They don't do this stuff when I get As on tests, but a league championship is a whole different thing. I nod and smile polite. "Thanks. Thanks a lot."

I am a big deal! Me. Regular Raymond Wisniewski. My name was even in *The Franklin Times Herald* this morning. With a picture! In color! I've got the article folded up in my wallet.

Raymond Wisniewski saved the day for the Red Storm, scoring the winning basket on a spinning drive down the lane in the final minute.

That was the best part of the article even though it was not accurate. We were already up by one when I scored, so it was not a winning basket. As far as spinning, the only thing spinning was my head, but I'll take it.

Suddenly Walter's big frame fills the doorway. He stands there a second staring, then a big smile breaks out on his face. He strides over and bear-hugs me. "My hero!"

"Hey! Hey!" I laugh.

Walter steps back. "Awesome, man! I was reading about you in the paper!" He is like a different person.

"Yeah. We just all played our game."

"Yeah, but you won it. You showed everybody how to play the game."

I can't tell if he's for real or not. "Right."

We sit down. Walter licks his lips. "I gotta tell you some-thing." He leans in close and talks low. "About that shop thing." He hangs his head. "Look. I didn't know I was gonna hit the guy. He pissed me off and I just swung. I didn't think about anything else. Like what was in my hand. You know that, right?"

"Yeah. I guess."

"No. For real. It was just—I wasn't thinking." He moves his hand through his hair. "And Stoshy told me he told you. I didn't know it was Stoshy. I thought—never mind."

He's really mellowed out. He's like normal. "Forget it." I reach out, and we shake hands. "Just don't flip any more tables on me."

He grins. "Yeah. I'll look for something bigger next time."

We head out into the hall and slap hands when we split off for our classes. As I round the corner another big football dude calls out, "Nice game." I give him a wave.

All day it goes like that. Walking down the hall to Spanish I feel like I'm glowing even though Spanish stinks now. I used to like Spanish. We would pretend we were in restaurants and order stuff, or at a train station trying to get the right train, but our new teacher, Mrs. Sigmund, has us trying to read this huge famous Spanish novel that none of us has a clue about.

"Hi."

It's a girl's voice. I look to my side. Stacey is there wearing this low-low-cut spaghetti strap top. She is bursting out of it. *Don't stare! Talk!*

"Hi."

"Ray. Congratulations. What a great game!" She puts a hand up for a high five. I high-five her. I can smell her perfume. She is definitely in my personal space. She pushes her hair back with her hand. Her chest swells out when she does. *Don't look!*

"Thanks, Stacey."

"Mind if I walk with you?"

Right! "No. Great. How are you?"

"I'm fine." She smiles. Her teeth are perfect. She's got pink lipstick on that is light enough to look good.

"So . . ."

I see Gerard walking on the opposite side of the hall. I smile and nod, letting him see *me* with Stacey. He bugs his eyes and pretends like he's fainting and holding on to the wall for support. This is excellent.

She moves her hair back again behind her ear with one hand and seems to be even closer now. I look at her chest again.

"I was telling my friends about you."

"Really? What were you saying?"

"You know, how we've known each other since kindergarten. About what a great player you are. How you tutor adults. After a while they were like, 'Stacey, shut up about Ray already.' "

She was talking about *me* to her friends! I shrug. "Ah, the whole team did great."

"But, you were, just like—Wow!"

I laugh. Now! Now is the time! Ask! Ask her out!

Sarah.

That's my next thought. *Sarah.* It's amazing how many things can flash around in your head at once. Sarah and I have just started talking and she kept having stuff come up when I asked her to see my games. I'm not even sure—

Stacey rests her fingers real lightly on my arm. "It's neat to have a chance to talk to you."

"Yeah." There is never going to be a better time to try this. Ever. I take a deep breath. "Stacey, I've been meaning to ask, would you ever want to go to a movie or something?" I almost cringe after it gets past my lips. Is she going to laugh?

"It's about time."

I try to breathe again. "You were waiting on me to ask you?"

"Of course! For months." She messes my hair up. "You are so thick." She giggles. "What time?"

What time? I hadn't thought it was possible. "You mean, what time tonight?"

"When did you mean?"

"Tonight! Tonight is good. Can I call you after school? I didn't pick a time, I mean, movie yet. I mean, you can pick a movie . . ."

"Here." She stops, slips my notebook out of my arms and

writes her phone number on the inside cover. Doesn't ask or anything. Just does it.

This is perfect. T gave us tonight off because of the win. As I walk into Spanish, Stacey touches my arm again and says, "You pick the movie. I don't care. Just call me right after school, okay?"

My heart is racing. I try to say okay, but all I can do is nod. I've got Stacey Steck's phone number! We're going out to a movie tonight! This is incredible! It's like I'm in some-one else's life. My name is on the sports page and I'm going out with Stacey Steck.

Spanish is a blur. The book doesn't bug me anymore. Suddenly it's a good book. Verb conjugation is good. Everything is good. I open my notebook and look at the phone number. It's big, loopy girl writing. In purple ink.

The bell rings and I get up to leave. Out in the hall I see Stacey talking to Hope. As I walk by, she reaches out and touches my arm again. I stop and stare at the perfect white teeth. The green, green eyes. Big full lips. Her hair is shining. Even Hope is smiling at me.

Stacey says, "Don't forget to call me."

Right. Like don't forget to breathe.

chapter twenty-three
MOVIE TIME

This is so incredible. I jog over to auto shop to see if Walter's there. I catch him outside the door talking with Teddy. Walter waves. "Here he is—superstar!"

I stop in front of him. "Walter. Check this out. I'm taking Stacey out tonight!"

He waves a big hand at me. "Get out."

"I'm serious."

He shakes his head. "No."

"Yeah!"

He takes a step back. "Whoa! You de man! Basketball star *and* love machine. That is so cool." He double high-fives me.

Teddy pretends he's pulling a train whistle. *"Wooo! Wooo!"*

Walter rubs his hands together. "Hey, maybe bring a video cam. Some girls are into that."

"You're sick, man." The bell rings. I've got one more class.

"Better get going before she wakes up and realizes she's going on a date with a total geek."

My face is starting to ache from smiling. I jog off to study hall. "Walter, I'll see you, man."

He waves. "Yeah. Don't do everything I wouldn't do."

When I get home I get ready for the most major event of my life. Look up the movie. Check the time. Call Stacey. She's not there. I leave a message with her little sister. Borrow my mother's car, clean the car, clothes selection, shower, hair-combing, deodorant, hair-combing again, more deodorant. I am doing everything twice to make sure it's right.

Finally I get in the little Toyota. It's either that or my dad's work van. I feel a little embarrassed about it because it's a scrubby little car, but it's better than walking. Stacey only lives three blocks over. Her house is the same as mine except her parents have made it all Victorian-looking with stained glass, brass lighting, and all that. When I get there, she's on her porch, sitting on the railing with her legs dangling. She's got on a powder blue ski jacket and tight jeans. Very tight. A white turtleneck is sticking out from the jacket. She looks like a model.

When she sees me, she jumps off the porch, jogs around the car, and hops in. "Hi!" she says. She tosses her hair back. *She is in my car!*

"Hi." Then I just blurt out what I'm thinking. "You look great." My whole body goes on red alert with her being squeezed next to me in a little car. The hairs on my arms stand up.

"Thanks." She gives me a big smile. "What are we going to see?"

I am inches away from an incredible, incredible body. What are we going to see? Someone erased my mind. "The, the one with the—"

"Oh, there's a good chance we'll be meeting up with Hope if everything works out—"

I don't have to answer about the movie. She keeps going. I can't even hear most of what she's saying because I'm concentrating on driving and still trying to deal with the fact that she is right next to me.

Finally, she takes a break and I sneak in a question. I want to get this one particular point ironed out before we get too far. "You know, Stacey, I've got to tell you. I'm a little surprised we're going out."

Her face goes slack. When she answers she sounds almost annoyed. "Really? Why?"

"Well, I thought you were going out with Brock." If this date is going to be a secret I want to be prepared in case Brock is coming to pound me and I need to duck behind stuff.

Her face goes back in position. She smiles. "We dated, but I like to do things with other people. Don't you?"

I smile. "Sure. Absolutely." She makes it sound so simple. Maybe it is.

After ten more minutes of hearing mostly about Hope, we're there. I get out and open her door. She takes my hand to get out of the little, low car. "Thanks, Ray."

I almost hold on to the hand, but then I figure don't push it. We cross the parking lot in silence. She's looking around. I move in front of her to get the lobby door. We walk through and I immediately hear my name. "Hey, Ray!"

I look and there's Winnie and Bernadette in line by the ticket guy just about to go in. Winnie waves and motions me over. I turn to Stacey. "It's Winnie and Bernadette." I take a step to head over.

Stacey doesn't move. "Oh. From the basketball team."

I stop too. "Yeah. Winnie. He's a nice guy."

"Oh yeah," she says. She puts her hands in her pockets. She's still standing right there.

"Yeah, I'm going to go say hi."

She doesn't move forward. I'm picking up a bad vibe here and I don't want to make a mistake. I try again. "Why don't we go over and see what's up?"

She whispers, "Oh. You know. I'd rather not." Then with a little apologetic smile she adds, "I'm not really good friends with Bernadette."

"Oh." I look back over and Bernadette and Winnie are still right there looking at us. Nobody's moving. It feels like minutes are ticking by. "I'm just going to go see . . ."

Stacey interrupts. "Wait. I was just thinking." She pauses. "I mean it's just a thought, but . . ." She quick scans the posters. "There's really not anything I have to see here. Maybe we should just go somewhere by ourselves instead."

She pauses. "My parents aren't home." She locks her eyes on me. "That could be fun."

Lightning charges through my body. There is instant sweat under my pits. My mind is racing. Winnie is watching me. I need to tell him quick and get going. "Wait here. I'll be right back."

I have to work real hard not to sprint across the lobby. Winnie slaps me five and grins. "Hey, man, Stacey Steck? You got a date with Stacey? Bring her over, let's sit together."

Bernadette slaps his arm. "Be quiet, Winnie. What are you going on about?" She starts imitating him, "Stacey Steck! Stacey Steck!"

I try not to look back, but I'm wondering what she's doing. "Well, uh, I got a little situation with Stacey."

"What? She won't let you get over?" Winnie laughs. Bernadette hits him again. He peers at her over my shoulder. "What's she doing? C'mon, we can sit together."

I whisper so Bernadette won't hear. "She told me she wants to go somewhere alone."

"She just said that now?"

"Yeah."

He looks hard at me. "You just walked in."

"Look, I don't know. All I know is we got here and now she wants to go somewhere else." I try to make my voice kind of light like, "Who knows with girls?"

Winnie doesn't say anything at first. Then he says, "Right. C'mon, Bern." He takes her arm and starts walking.

I say, "I'll see you around, right?"

"Yeah, sure. Diss me and go." Bernadette looks off into space.

"What? Hey, she wants to do something else now. I think I better do something else now, y'know?"

"Screw you," he says over his shoulder.

"What?"

Bernadette says, "Stop it, Winnie! Ray, we'll catch you another time." She grabs his arm and pulls him along.

This is not good at all. I look at Stacey and she's there reading the posters. I walk back. I try to be casual. I smile and shrug. "Uh, Stace. I think they'd really like us to join them."

She just looks at me. "I thought we were going to my house."

"Yeah, but . . ."

She threads her arm through mine. "Look. They've already gone in." She tightens her grip and leans her chest against me. The lightning shoots through me again. Then I look and see Winnie at the last second as they're heading in the door. He gives me a look that is supercold. Bernadette glances over too. She just looks sad. My stomach sinks. The lightning is gone.

They hand their tickets to the guy and disappear into the dark. Stacey says, "Come on. Let's go."

We walk across the lobby, through the door, and into the parking lot. I stop. What am I doing? I slip my arm out of hers, as casually as I can.

She frowns. "I'm sorry. Was I too pushy with that?"

"No, it's—"

She says, "I mean my friends could be here any minute. Hope would flip."

I am in stunned silence. I've got to make sure I've got this right. "You've got a problem going into a movie with Bernadette and Winnie?"

"Yeah?" She says it like "Duh!"

"Because?"

"You know."

This is not all fitting together. "I thought you were president of the Multicultural Club."

Her eyes flash angrily. "That's school. That's not double-dating in public, Ray."

"Oh."

She starts talking to me like I'm slow on the uptake and need a little more elementary explanation, but she's smiling again. "Look. If you want to get into Harvard or Yale or any Ivy, you have to have the grades, the test scores, be well rounded, do activities, organizations. All that, right?"

I just listen.

"But it can't just be any kind of organization or activity. Girl Scouts or whatever doesn't cut it anymore. Everybody does that. You need something like 'Multicultural' or 'Gay/Lesbian' in the title. You know? You get that on your application, everything else being equal, you're the one who gets in." She wrinkles her forehead. "Just the way of the world, honey."

"Stacey! Stacey!"

Stacey whirls around. "Oh. There's Hope! I'll be right back." She waves and calls back, "Hi!" It's like Hope is the president.

Stacey scoots across the parking lot. I see Winnie's face and Bernadette's face again in my head like on instant replay. Winnie's mad eyes. Bernadette's sad mouth. I watch Stacey chattering and laughing with Hope and two other girls. They see me looking and they all wave. I give a weak wave back. I am gonna be sick. I know what I have to do.

After a minute Stacey jogs back to me with a huge smile. She's all bubbly. "I told them you and I were going somewhere else. They're cool with it." She smiles and grabs my arm and entwines it with hers again. "They know you're an irresistible hunk." She tosses her hair and in this make-believe high voice says, "Hope was a little bit jealous, I think."

I have to clear my throat. I have trouble talking. "Stacey. You know. This is really weird, but I think you better go see what's up with your friends."

Now it's her turn to look stunned. "Why?"

"Actually, I'm not feeling so good." I can't look at her. "I can still drive you home if you want."

She takes it in for a second. "Are you sure?"

Am I sure? I guess I am. "Yeah."

She gets it. She lets go. Real quick she says, "That's okay, Ray. I'm sorry you don't feel well. Don't worry, I'll get a ride with them." She is a good actress.

"Sorry, Stacey."

She bounces off. "Don't worry about it. We'll do it again another time."

"Yeah. Sure."

"Definitely. See you at school. Feel better!" She even smiles.

I stand there for a second. Maybe more like ten. She's not bothered at all. Meanwhile, I feel like I'm carrying chains on my back. I wander back out to the car. I'm already behind the wheel before I realize it. I stare out the windshield for a minute feeling numb. Then I drive.

Sometimes driving feels really good. It's almost mindless. I turn the heater up because suddenly I feel cold. I get on the interstate, so I can just cruise and not worry about lights or stop signs.

I see Bernadette's face again. And Winnie's—so mad—like he hated me. You think Winnie would figure it out and let it slide. It wasn't about him. It was about Stacey. He knows I'm not like that.

Then again. Why would he think I'm not like that—if I just acted like that.

I can hear the highway hum by underneath my feet. Just that hummm. I replay the scenes tonight different ways, but it doesn't matter. It's too late. I insulted Winnie and Bernadette. Two really nice people. I blew them off because of a stupid girl.

I drive the fifteen miles to Pennsylvania, take the first exit over the river, and loop back. The river is all big and black under the bridge. Big and black and empty.

I messed up. Like my dad had warned me not to. I let my little head do my thinking for my big head.

chapter twenty-four
STAY OUT OF MY WAY

I am not looking forward to school today. I wonder how much Stacey told her friends about Friday. Probably nothing. She just wanted to say she went out with me. It's Winnie I'm concerned with. I know I'm going to see him in Paterson's class. I don't know what I'm going to say, but I want to say something.

When I walk into the cafeteria, there's Walter all smiles. He yells across the room, "Hey, Stud! Did you get over?"

Heads turn. I look out the windows, pretending he's not talking to me. When I sit down he starts giggling. "So, what happened? Details. I want details!"

I want to keep this short. "It didn't work out."

He throws his hands in the air in anguish. "What do you mean?"

"We didn't get along."

His voice goes all high. "How can you not get along with *that*?"

There'll be no explaining it to Walter. "We're too different."

"You couldn't make an exception? You know. Work out your *differences*."

I move my books around. "It's just—she's pretty cold."

"She's cold? C'mon."

"It was not good. Trust me."

Walter shakes his head. "Un-real."

I change the subject. "So, anyway, you're still, like, cooled out, right?"

Walter smiles. "Will you forget that? I am like a cucumber."

I relax a little. "I always said you were a vegetable."

"You ditch Stacey Steck and I'm the vegetable? Think again." He swats at me and I rap him back hard on the shoulder. "Anyway, you still got your first love."

"Who's that?"

"Basketball, man. I'm even gonna catch your game Friday, now that you're a big hero and stuff. See you teach these brothers how to play the game."

I don't like the last remark, but everything else is so normal, I don't want to rock the boat right away. "Yeah. Okay. I'll get you a seat in the skybox."

When I get to Paterson's class Winnie's not in his seat. But Sarah looks up and I give her a little wave. She waves back so I stop at her desk. She's got on a red and white candy-striped sweater. "Hi," she says. "How are you?"

"Okay. How about you?"

She looks down. "Fine."

"Anything going on?"

"No. Not really." She looks up again and real bouncy says, "How was your date with Stacey?" I am immediately very aware that I really, really didn't want Sarah to know about this. But she does.

Winnie walks in and goes right by me. He sits down, takes out his notebook, and starts reading. Now, this is complete perfection. Really fine. Winnie and Bernadette think I'm a jerk. Stacey used me. And Sarah knows I went out with someone else. I don't know where to look. I manage an "Okay."

"That's great." She's smiling, but she's looking right past me. Seeing her eyes like that, all disconnected, hurts.

"Sarah, I—"

Paterson says, "Let's get started, people."

I sit down, but I don't hear one word Paterson says. I've got two people I care about, right in front of me, pissed at me. I don't even know who to try to fix things up with first. After class I follow Sarah into the hall. "Sarah."

She stops. Her two friends stop, look at me, then keep walking.

"About that date. It was a—what's the word—'disaster'? 'Debacle'?"

She says, "Oh?" Then starts walking again.

"Listen. Can I talk to you? We can go to the library. Just for a minute."

She hesitates. "I don't think so. I really have to go."

"Just for a minute. Okay?" She isn't moving. She looks at her feet. "Sarah, I'd really appreciate it."

She looks away down the hall. "No, I don't—"

"Please."

She hesitates but finally nods. "Okay."

I follow her to the back of the library. She slides carefully into a big chair. I sit down right across from her. I clear my throat and tell her the whole sickening little story from beginning to end. She listens to it all without saying a word. I figure now she's going to get up and say, "You jerk. I thought you liked me. I wrote you a love poem. Get lost." Instead she says, "I don't have any black friends."

That's a real interesting comment and a heck of a lot better than what I expected. I'm caught a little off guard but I manage to talk again. "I didn't either, really, till basketball. Probably never would have, if it hadn't been for that. Also got me my worst enemy."

"Really? Who?"

"Robert Peyton."

"I don't think I know him."

"No, you probably wouldn't know Robert. He's a little guy, real dark, with a shaved head. Do you know what Coach has us doing?" I'm so glad we're talking about something else besides me and Stacey.

"What?"

"Coach T has him working with me on ballhandling.

Robert hates me, but Coach pairs us up to work out every day. Just the two of us." I keep going and tell her all about Robert in tryouts, in ROCK with Tyrone, our fight in tutorial, his trying to set me up for the drug thing.

"You think he hates you?"

"Definitely."

She pushes her glasses up. Her eyes are really brown. Deep brown, but sparkly. "Why?"

I lower my voice. "I guess because I'm white. He hates Pruze too. He tried to get us thrown off the team."

"So, he likes all the black kids on the team?"

I have to think about that. "Well, no. I mean, I don't know. He's not friends with Winnie."

"So maybe it's not just about black and white."

I don't know what to say. I never thought about that. "Yeah. Could be."

"Do you want to know what I think?" she says.

I'm amazed this quiet little girl has all this to say. I wonder if all the other quiet girls in my classes are full of stuff like this waiting to jump out. "Yeah, of course."

"I think he doesn't like you because he's selfish. He's immature."

I picture Robert like a little kid, like a baby with a diaper on. "What do you mean?"

"You don't do what he wants you to do. Neither did that guy Tyrone you talked about. He's spoiled. He wants his way. He expects it, like a child."

I just nod. "I never thought about it that way, but you might be right." Sarah is a deep girl. "Sarah, if I ever need a psychiatrist, I'll have to call you. I'll lay on your couch and you can analyze me."

"Would you really like to lie on my couch?"

I feel my eyes get wide. She has this little smile, and her eyes are very playful-looking. The glasses look so cute. I didn't know smart, quiet girls could tease around like this.

"Absolutely." I feel my heart leap up in my chest. I lean forward. "Can I lie on your couch?"

"It's 'may I?', and maybe we should just go out to a movie or something first."

I look down at our feet. I have my huge white hightops on. She's wearing these little brown tassel loafers and pink socks.

"Well then . . ." I take a big dramatic pause, "Do you want to go out Saturday?" Which is what I should have asked her a long time ago and it would have saved me a whole lot of trouble.

"Sure," she says smiling.

The bell for class rings, so I stand up. "All right. You know I was going to ask. Remember I asked about those games? I was just getting warmed up."

She stands up too. "Uh-huh. Sure." She's grinning. "Call me. We're in the phone book."

"You got it." We walk out together and wave an awkward

good-bye. Girls are hard to figure. Or maybe it's just people in general.

We have one more regular season game before the state tournament starts. Now that we've got the league won, tomorrow's game doesn't matter much, but we're playing Gloucester City, which is a good team. They're one of only two teams that beat us, but they're inconsistent because they rely on this one guy, Charlie Gould. He's pretty incredible. When he's hot, they win. When he's not, they lose.

After lunch, which I didn't eat because I was talking to Sarah, I head to Calculus. Walking by the school store, I see Winnie hanging with D-Man. I've got to do this right now. I call over as I walk, "Hey, Winnie."

D-Man grins and says, "Whup! Here he is. Playboy! You get nice wit' Stacey?"

I roll my eyes. "Yeah, right."

Winnie hops off the ledge and immediately walks away. "Hey. Wait up."

I know he hears me, but he keeps on walking. D-Man says, "He's pissed, man. You dissed him somethin' bad."

I walk fast and catch up. "Winnie."

He's not talking. His shirttails are out and flying, he's moving that quick. I lean over so he has to see me. "Hey, c'mon. Think about it. The most beautiful girl in the whole school! How many chances am I going to get like that?"

Winnie talks to the air. "Bug off, Ray." He's got this fierce look in his eyes.

"What? She didn't want to hang with you guys. It's not a big thing. She doesn't like Bernadette."

"Right. She didn't want to hang with *us guys*."

He just keeps striding ahead. I'm right next to him. I say, "I didn't even go to the movie with her. I went home."

"You're my hero."

I stop. "Hey, cut me a break here."

He finally stops too. He says all flat, like he's giving instructions. "I don't want to hear it. Just stay out of my way."

"That's right. Stay out of his way!" It's Rudy. He's right there in front of us wearing a jerky lime green shirt and dark green pants. He looks like a big asparagus. "You hang with the whiteys. Stay out the soul brothers' way!" He dances around and puts a bony hand on Winnie's shoulder walking him over to a group of black guys by the bathroom.

Winnie doesn't look back and he doesn't take Rudy's hand off.

chapter twenty-five
WHITE IS RIGHT!

We aren't practicing well. Coach has us running stuff and then running it again, but everybody is just off somehow. It's all a letdown till the states, but we have to play this last game. Winnie and I keep avoiding each other. He plays normal on the court in practice, passing me the ball and everything, but he has nothing to say to me and I'm not going to go begging.

We jog out on the floor for warm-ups in front of a big crowd. Everybody's here to see the new league champs. Stacey gives me a wave and a big smile from the sidelines, like nothing ever happened.

Gloucester City wins the tap and turns it into an easy breakaway layup. Then Charlie Gould hits four straight jumpers over the top of our zone.

Gould is their man. He's a white guy about my size who's balding and always looks like he needs a shave. Pruze says he's really forty and has three kids at home, but Charlie can shoot. And he's doing it tonight. He's very quick. As soon as the ball touches his hands, he's up in the air shooting.

Coach T calls time. "We're switching the defense. Box and one. Raymond, you take Gould. Deny him the jumper. Make him drive."

"Okay, Coach." I go out and D up hard against Gould. First time down he has the ball, I move in tight. He bends his knees and starts his motion. I leap up to jam it, but there's nobody there. He's by me already, pulling up, hitting the short J. Then he does it again. And then again. He's like lightning.

I feel like a sack of lead with feet. This guy is using me up in front of everybody. I think about Winnie. I look over at Stacey cheering. My concentration is less than good. There's no helmet on tonight.

T pulls me out. It's the first time in my life I've ever been glad to be pulled out. D-Man goes in for me.

"Five Spades!"

It's Rudy. He's clapping and chanting again. "Five Spades! Whoop! Whoop! Five Spades! Whoop! Whoop!" The same crowd is joining in again too. There's maybe six guys doing it, but they're loud. Me, Pruze, and Ziggy are off. An all-black team, that's what they're digging.

T is talking to me. He says, "Sit down, Raymond, and watch Gould. He usually goes to his right to shoot. Try to overplay him that way. I want you to work with Al—" The words bounce off of me. All I can hear is Rudy screeching. "Five Spades! Five Spades!"

Pruze goes back in and Rudy and crew boo him. Pruze

makes this wacky face at them with his tongue hanging out. Coach T yells, "Pruzakowski! Play the game!"

It goes like that the whole first half. Rudy's little crowd boos me, Pruze, and Ziggy every time we're on. They're booing us! Their own team. It catches on some too, with other kids yelling it and booing. Nobody's hitting and we go down twelve. At halftime, T lays out a counterattack, but I still can't focus.

Five minutes into the second half, I go back in. *Boom! Boom! Boom!* When I look I see Walter and Teddy with four or five other guys all standing and stomping their work boots on the bleachers. They're chanting, "White is right! We're gonna fight! White is right! We're gonna fight!" Walter promised to see the game. And here he is for the second half. Perfect.

Walter bellows over to Rudy's group, "We need some white boys with brains to tell you savages what to do!"

Rudy yells back, "Shut up, honky!"

The people in the middle are yelling at them to sit down. Finally some of the teachers get up there to cool it off. Meanwhile I'm doing everything except wrestling Gould to the ground, while he hits without even looking. He's totally unconscious.

On top of that, every time I sit down, Rudy's boys cheer and when I go in, Walter and company are yelling, "White is right!" and stomping. Suddenly it's all about me and I'm having the worst game of my life. I foul out with five minutes left. I'm embarrassed beyond belief. At the end, Gould has thirty-two points and we lose by ten. We shuffle to the locker room.

"Hey!"

I look up. Rudy is walking along on the bleachers following me. "Nice defense there, Raymond Whitey!" His little bunch cackle like it's the funniest thing ever.

I jump up one row, two rows. I grab Rudy by the front of his shirt. He pulls back, yelling, "Hey! Hey!"

Big arms wrap around me from behind. "C'mon, George Foreman. Save it for later," Pruze says.

I let go of Rudy. He loses his balance and falls on the bleacher, but then bounces up screaming, "Touch *me*! Touch *me*!"

Coach T is right there. He scowls at both of us. "Get in the locker room. Now!"

Rudy straightens his shirt out. He points at me as I walk away and yells, "Mess with *me*! You gonna get hurt, Raymond Whitey. Count on it!"

Coach glances up there again, then walks behind us.

In the locker room, it's dead quiet. T stands there staring at us for a second and then says, "Find a seat in the team room." The team room is a little room inside the locker room for meetings. Everyone drags in. T closes the door. I figure now we're going to hear it. We stunk. Especially me.

He puts a foot up on a bench and rests both arms on his knee. In a low voice he says, "Boys. This was a tough game.

I don't have to tell you, you never got on track. Next time it's the states and another slip like this and our season is over." T is so cool. No yelling. Just tells it like it is.

Guys look all over, at the floor, their shoes, the lockers. He pauses. "I know you heard the crowd again tonight."

All eyes flip up and on him. Nothing is moving.

"And I need to address it." He walks slowly to the center and folds his arms. "Unfortunately we've got some vocal individuals around here who have made themselves somewhat of a distraction."

He moves slowly to the other side of the room. "They tend to have pretty narrow views about people. For example, to this type of individual, a black person is and does certain things. If they don't—they're not *really* black."

He walks the other way. "And a white person, of course, is and does certain other things."

He stops. "You'll find with these people that if you deviate from their definition of who you are supposed to be, what you are supposed to do, they may well get angry. Abusive. Sometimes even violent. Either through ignorance, hate, or willfulness. It doesn't matter. The effect is the same." He pauses and dusts some fuzz off his pants. "But you have to ask yourself, despite the consequences, am I ever going to let others define who I am?"

He paces again, stopping by the door. "I put this question to you because at some point, you will most likely have to answer it." He and Robert are looking right at each other.

"Maybe soon." Then he swings his eyes and looks right at me. I look down. "You're going to have to decide who is going to define you." No one says anything. "It is my hope you will have the courage to define yourselves."

No one moves.

"Any questions?"

All you can hear is breathing. "One last thing then. I'd like to read you a quote. Sort of a prayer, if you don't mind. I think it's appropriate for us as a team at this time."

He takes out a folded up piece of yellow paper from his wallet. He opens it and reads slowly rolling each word out. "Grant us brotherhood. Not only for this day, but for all our years." He pauses and scans the room. I catch Winnie looking at me, then away. "A brotherhood not of words—but of acts—and deeds."

It's dead silent. "Gentlemen, think about it," he says almost in a monotone. "We will practice tomorrow morning at eight sharp." He takes the little yellow paper and tacks it onto the announcement board.

No one says much of anything after that. Even Pruze is quiet. The lockers don't bang and there's no singing in the showers. I leave through the side door by myself, and there's Walter waiting out in the parking lot by his truck like I figured. He comes walking toward me. "Hey, my man. Tough game, but it was dynamite seeing you go after that punk, Rudy."

I am so damn frustrated. I push him. Hard. He rocks back on his feet. I yell, "Didn't we talk about this?"

He pushes me right back. Real hard. I bang back against the hood.

"What?" he says.

I straighten right up. "You know what! You said you were cool." A couple of people near another car stop and look over.

"What? I'm supposed to sit there and let those goons do all that Five Spades crap?"

"Yes! Let *them* look like idiots."

"Let them call you 'Raymond Whitey'? Boo you?" Walter shakes his head. "You got to stop putting up with all these black—"

I cut him off short. "I got friends who are black. Friends on this team."

He spreads his arms out. "Friends?" He spits the word out. "Name one of your *friends* who stood up for you tonight."

I start to say Winnie, but what could he have done? When I don't say anything, Walter keeps going, "*I* stood up for you. The brothers stick together. We got to stick together. You know that old Sly and the Family Stone song? 'Family Affair'?"

Walter starts singing and rocking. "Blood's thicker than mud. It's a family affair." He pauses. "You know what that's about?"

"What are you—"

He moves his hands around as he talks. "The mud is supposed to be Woodstock in '69, you know how it rained and was all muddy, but everybody was having peace and love and all, blacks and whites and all whoever. Well old Sly, he's black too. He says, by the way, when it comes down to it, all this peace and love is BS. When it comes down to it, the *blood* is thicker than the *mud*."

I just stare.

"He means blacks stick with blacks and whites stick with the whites. That's why they call each other 'blood' sometimes."

"That's real deep."

Walter spits. "Yeah. You think you're so smart. There's a lot of stuff you don't have a clue about."

This is going nowhere. "Walter. I mean it. Lay off it. Don't pull this crap again."

Walter looks at me. He takes a deep breath. Then he tries to act all casual stretching his arms up over his head and yawning. "Okay. Fine. Let's go. I'm freezing my butt off out here."

When he stretches his arms, his sleeves hike up and I spot something on his forearm. A small blue tattoo on a background of red flame. "What's on your arm?"

Walter laughs a weird forced chuckle. "Nothing." He pulls his sleeve back down.

"Was that a swastika?"

"None of your business." He glares at me.

"*That* is whacked."

"Hey. It's about white solidarity. Something you don't know a lot about."

"Yeah? Show it to the old guys in the neighborhood. They'll take your 'white solidarity' off you with a butter knife."

Walter says, "Don't worry about me. What are you all freaked out about anyway? Teddy drew it. It's not even real. C'mon, let's go."

"I'm out of here." I start walking.

Walter calls after me. "Don't be stupid. Get in."

"No. I'll see you."

Then he yells, "I'm not good enough for you now?"

I call back over my shoulder. "I feel like walking."

I hear the truck start. The tires grind across the gravel. The rumbling comes up next to me. Walter looks down at me from the window. "Walk then, asshole."

And he takes off.

chapter twenty-six

SEVEN

It's quiet in the locker room. It might be that it's eight o'clock on a Saturday morning, but I don't know. I feel like crap after last night's game and my talk with Walter.

Then Al calls out from down the row of lockers as we're putting on our practice gear, "Hey, Pruze!"

"Yeah, man?" Pruze calls back.

"Talk some Polish to me, man!"

"Całować się mi!" Pruze yells.

Al walks over to me and leans down. "What's that mean, Ray? Is that a curse, man?" He looks at Pruze, making his eyes like slits and curls his lip. "Sounds like a curse. You best not be cursin' me you big, fat Polish pickle!"

I'm real glad Al walked over. "Nah. In Polish it means, give me a kiss."

"What!" Al looks like he's going to gag. Then he yells to Pruze, "You sick, man! You sick, Pruze!"

Pruze laughs so hard he starts choking. He stumbles out onto the court. I follow and get under the basket with him. I push into him pretending I'm trying to get a spot to shoot from.

"Hey, Shaq."

"Hey, Pruze."

Pruze pushes back with his butt and shoots a turnaround. It goes right in. "You talk to Walter yet?"

"Yeah. I thought he was pretty straight till last night. Then that Five Spades crap set him off." I remember the little red and blue swastika.

"I'll say. I saw your man, Walter, in the hallway right after the game, and he's blowing a gasket at me. He tells me he's gonna come to my house and get me."

"For what?"

"Right. That's what I asked. He says because I pulled you off Rudy. He says I'm betraying my race, he's gonna straighten me out, he's tired of us getting pushed around. Psycho stuff."

My stomach drops when I hear that. T blows the whistle and we line up. I keep an eye on Winnie, but he isn't looking. Robert is, though. Which is funny. I catch him looking a couple of times during practice. Robert is usually real purposeful in ignoring me, but he's definitely checking me out.

On Monday, Walter doesn't show at our table in the cafeteria. I don't take that as a good sign. Winnie is not talking, but I think he nodded at me in Paterson's class as I walked by his desk. I nodded back. Maybe it's a start.

Sarah is absent, which is really unfortunate because she's the only person I feel I could actually talk to about Walter. Which says something about me and Sarah already.

Practice is okay. After practice, though, it's tutorial as usual. T hasn't let us stop even after my dazzling dribbling against Yorkville. Hah! I catch Robert doing that same looking thing again. He's not saying anything, but he's looking at me a lot.

After tutorial I do my foul shooting, while I wait for Robert to clear out. The warm shower feels excellent. I start to mellow out a little. It's been bitter cold, but the weather report says it's supposed to be warming up. A little spring breaking in. I hope so. I'm getting tired of wearing all these clothes. I put on a flannel shirt, a sweater over that, and my ski jacket so I'm looking like the Michelin Man.

I come out of the locker room into the hall. It's empty except for some guys hanging out by the school store, black clatch territory. That's what Pruze calls it. As I get closer I see it's Rudy, Robert, and Seven. You don't actually see Seven much in school. I look the other way and stay on the opposite side of the hall.

I'm almost to the door when a thin, disinterested voice calls over, "Hey, I wanna talk to you." It's Seven!

I think about hustling out the door, but since Rudy and Robert are watching, I stop and wait. Seven comes pimping over all cool. Robert stands up and says something I can't hear because Rudy's yelling something at the same time.

Seven shoots a punch that catches me right in the side of the jaw like a hammer. My head rocks back and I hit the door and go down to the tile floor. I am seeing fireworks but as I'm going down I also see a shiny, black, pointy shoe coming at me. I grab his pant cuff and pull. The one foot he still has on the ground slides out and he falls hard on the tile. "Stupid mother!" he growls.

I get to one knee and scramble to push the door open. I know there's kids on the other side waiting for late buses. Got to get their attention. Seven grabs my leg, but I fall through. The door opens.

And there's Malovic running toward us. "Hey!" he yells.

He rushes through the door and grabs me by an arm and Seven by an arm and hoists us up. First time I've ever been glad to see Malovic. Kids from the bus stop are crowding behind him.

Malovic yells at them, "Back outside! Go ahead."

Mr. Feder, the chemistry teacher, comes in from the parking lot. He's a pretty big guy. "You got it, Pete?"

Malovic is holding tight on my arm. "Yes. It's fine."

"What happened?"

"Little tussle. I'll take care of it."

Mr. Feder herds people out the door. "All right. Everybody outside. Let's go."

Seven tries to pull his arm away. "Get off me. I didn't do nuthin'." Malovic jerks him off the ground a little. He's stronger than I thought. And he looks mad. He starts pulling us down the hall. Rudy and Robert are nowhere around.

So this is why Robert has been checking me out. He was thinking all about setting me up. This is his little plot. And now he's faded off into the distance like the little chicken he is.

Seven gets put into the principal's office with the assistant principal, Mr. Gallo. Malovic puts me in his office. "Are you okay?"

I nod and sit down. He goes into a little fridge and gets me an ice pack. "I saw everything, Raymond. I know Tracey started it."

"Tracey?" Now that things are calm, I notice my jaw throbbing.

"The boy who hit you. Tracey West."

So that's Seven's real name. Malovic gets up and closes the door. He moves kind of slow. His white shirt is wrinkled and his tie is loose. "Raymond, do you have any idea why Tracey started in after you?"

"I don't know. I've never talked to him before in my life."

He sits down at his desk. "So, no reason you know of?"

"No." I press the ice pack against my jawbone. I hope it's not broken. I probably can't play with a broken jaw. I check my teeth with my tongue.

Malovic picks up a pencil and starts writing on a yellow pad. "Was anyone else involved?"

"Robert and Rudy were with him."

He stops writing and squints at me. "I didn't see them."

"It was right before you got there."

He fidgets in his chair and glances at the clock. "You're sure?"

"Yeah."

He looks back at me and frowns. "Where'd they go?"

"I don't know."

He motions with empty hands and suddenly he's sarcastic. "So, they just disappeared?"

The pain from my jaw shoots up the side of my head. "I don't know where they went."

He writes something on his pad, then talks to me real solemn. "It's a very serious matter to accuse anyone of being part of this."

"I didn't say they were part of this."

"You said they were with Tracey."

I don't say anything. Just look out the little window in his door.

He puts the pencil down. It's dead quiet. He leans forward. "Raymond. I want you to understand. You saying that they were involved is very serious."

I've had it. I'm hurting and sweating and I actually yell. "I didn't say they were involved! You asked was anyone else there! I'm telling you they were there!"

"Don't raise your voice!"

I just look away. It stays quiet while he breathes hard through his nose and looks at some papers on his desk. Finally I ask, "Can I get going?"

It's like he didn't hear me. "You know prejudice is a very terrible thing."

I am so sick of this man. I stand up. "A black kid hits me in the jaw for no reason and now I'm prejudiced?"

Snap! He leans back in his chair and smiles. His whole mood changes like that. He's all relaxed now. "Sit down," he says through the smile. He waits till I'm seated again then he says all teacherly, "Why'd you have to say a *black* kid hit you, Ray?" He lets that sink in. "Would you have said, 'An Asian kid hits me in the jaw'? Or, 'A white kid hits me in the jaw'?"

This jerk is twisting things so it sounds like I'm the bad guy somehow. Still, why did I say that? "I was just describing him."

"But I know what he looks like. You didn't need to describe him."

The pain is hammering on my temple. "I'm not prejudiced."

"That's what you say. But I've known you for a long time. I also know your good friend, Walter Wasko. I'm very aware of the kinds of belief systems you kids in Greenville have."

"You don't know anything about me."

He frowns and pauses, moving the pencil from hand to hand. "Do you remember when I offered you that spot as manager on the team? Remember what happened that morning? You came in. I could see it on your face. You were ready to join us. Then—you saw Robert. It dawned on you that you would be in a supporting role to an African American and you realized you couldn't handle that."

"Not 'cause he's African American. 'Cause he's a jerk!"

"You don't know Robert—"

This is beginning to come together for me. This is what it's all about with me and Malovic. "That's why you kept me off the team, isn't it? You think I'm a racist!"

He puts the fingertips of his hands together in front of his chest. "Not at all." He pauses. "Your ability. Experience. Attitude. The team mix. A variety of reasons."

"But my attitude? My racist attitude is one of your reasons?"

He pauses. "Honestly? Yes. Your attitude was a factor."

"Do you know I've got friends on this team who are black?"

He smiles at me. He shakes his head and starts chuckling. He catches his breath and sighs. He points his pencil at me. "You think because you play some basketball with a few African American students you aren't prejudiced?"

Everything on his desk is in neat little stacks: files, index cards, different colored note papers. I want to pick it all up and hurl it in his face. I push my chair back to get up. "You don't know anything about me! And something else—these kids are making a huge sucker out of you!"

He gets red instantly. "You have no understanding of what I've done with students under my supervision. Robert has serious academic challenges. Rudy—"

"Yeah? So does Walter! You know his father knocks him around? You know Walter works his ass off day and night? You know he's failing and all he needs is some tutoring and he would do all right? Why don't you help him? Aren't you his counselor too?"

"I help anyone who—"

I lean forward. "Oh, wait. I see." I point at him like he did to me. "It's 'cause he's from Greenville!" I tilt my head. "Are *you* prejudiced against kids like us from Greenville? Maybe you need to examine your own belief system, Mr. Malovic."

Malovic's face creases up like he's going to blast me good, but there's a polite little knock at the door. Mr. Gallo pokes his head in. Me and Malovic get quiet. "Excuse me, Pete."

Malovic straightens up in his chair. "Yes?"

"I just finished talking to a couple of students who said they saw the fight from inside the art room. They said there were a couple more kids with Tracey just before the incident."

"Who are the kids?"

"Rudy Robinson and Robert Peyton."

Malovic shoots a glance at me like he's daring me to say anything. Then he looks back to Gallo. "What does Tracey say about that?"

"He's not saying anything."

Malovic stares up at the clock. Gallo clears his throat. "Do you want me to make the calls?"

He stands up. "I will call them. Thank you."

Mr. Gallo leaves, but Malovic holds the door open. He gives me a very bad look. Like he tasted something he doesn't like. "You may go, Raymond. If I need you further, I'll let you know. But remember what I said. Prejudice is a very dangerous thing."

I try to stay cool as I walk past him and out. "Yeah. Don't I know it."

chapter twenty-seven
TURNING A CORNER

The next day at school my jaw is sore, but I've been hurt worse playing football. I told my mother and father it was from an elbow at practice.

No Walter in the cafeteria. What are we gonna say anymore anyway? I guess he figures the same. I walk out and head to the bathroom. Al is in the hall.

"Hey, man. I heard what happened. Let me see your jaw." I turn my head. It's a little blue, that's all. Not even swollen now. Al shakes his head. "Dang. Seven. They say he's getting expelled. Out on his butt this time."

"That would be okay with me."

Al laughs. "You okay. You got a hard head. Not as hard as Pruze, but hard enough."

I'm real glad to hear about Seven. It's pretty scary to think he might be around to try again.

In Paterson's class, Winnie glances over once, like to see what I'm doing in my notebook, but that's it. It's pretty uncomfortable sitting there within three feet of each other, not looking or saying anything.

On the way out of class, Sarah and I fall into step right next to each other. She peers at me through the wire rims. "Hi. How are you?"

"Hi. Okay."

"I heard you were in a fight."

How does she hear this stuff? I can't picture girls like Sarah talking about who cheerleaders are dating and fights that jocks and hoodlums are having, but I guess they do.

"Well, not even a fight. One punch in the jaw was all."

"Really?" She raises her eyebrows. "Are you okay?"

"Yeah, I'm fine. How about if I call you tonight? I'll fill you in."

She smiles real nice. "Good. I'd like that."

This warm feeling spreads across my chest. "Yeah. Me too."

"I'm going to go. I'll talk to you later." She reaches back and gives my hand a quick squeeze then scoots ahead to catch up with her friends. I really like this girl.

I head to my locker to get my lunch. As I get close I can see Walter leaning right next to it. He spots me and puts on a weird smile. Definitely forced. "Here he is!" he announces.

"Hey." I walk by him. I spin the combination.

"Been waitin' for ya." He leans over me. "So. How's b-ball?"

I don't look. "Great."

"Must be. Get your shoes shined in there real well I bet."

I smack the locker door and turn on him. "Knock it off, damn it! I told you!"

Walter backs up and puts his hands in the air all exaggerated. "Whoah! I'm kidding. Geez. Guy can't take a little joke."

People are looking. I lower my voice. "Hey. You wanna be that way—be that way. But I don't want to hear it."

Walter narrows his eyes. "I *said* I was jokin'."

We stand staring at each other. Walter puts his hands in his jeans pockets. I pull the locker door open. "Do you want something?"

"I think we should go to Howard's for some ice cream after dinner. To talk."

Howard's is a little place in Franklin that makes its own ice cream. "I don't think so."

He moves closer. "I said I want to talk to you."

I get out my lunch and my afternoon books. "Go ahead."

"Not here. I've got to get something off my chest, you know. About this stuff."

I look at him. In the eyes. I can't read anything. I don't say anything. I put my books and notebooks in order.

Walter leans back in against the locker and lets out a deep sigh. "Come on." He lowers his voice. "Don't bust my chops. I want to settle this."

He's asking. I can't just blow him off. I close the locker and spin the combo. "All right."

He smiles a thin smile. "Good. I'll get you about nine. It'll be great. Like old times." He claps me hard on the shoulder and moves off grinning.

Practice is hard. We work on breaking the press a lot. We do it again and again and again. I'm getting ready to say something to Winnie, but also hoping he'll say something first. Anyway, we spend another day not talking to each other. Robert is not at practice. Which is very unusual. Maybe they've already suspended his butt.

On my way out I think about Walter and tonight. What can I say to him? Hey, Walter. Stop being a racist. Be the nice, funny guy you used to be with me.

I wish I had somebody to talk to about it. Then I figure, maybe I do. So, I make a left instead of a right and head over to Sarah's.

It's such a cool neighborhood. With all the trees and shadows, it's real calming. I knock on her door. Fortunately, she answers. I hate dealing with girls' parents. They always look at you like you're a serial killer before they get to know you.

"Hi, Ray." She pushes her glasses up on her nose. She's got on a pink T-shirt, jeans, and mismatched socks, one yellow, one green.

"Hi, Sarah."

There's a little half smile on her face. "This is a surprise. I thought you were going to call."

"Well, I was in the neighborhood, so I figured I'd stop."

She gives me the eye. "In the neighborhood, huh?" She opens the door and moves aside. "Come on in."

"Well, within a five-mile radius. Thanks."

"Sure. Let's sit in here." She leads me into a room with a fireplace and bookshelves lining the walls. We sit on these big leather chairs with the little brass nail heads all over them. "Would you like anything? A soda?"

"No thanks."

She looks at me all expectant. I've got to start somewhere. I get ready to tell her all about Walter. When Malovic said how Walter and I are prejudiced, I knew he was half right. Maybe even more than half right. Instead I say, "So, how are you?"

She smiles. "I'm fine."

"Good. That's good." I try to get into it again, but as I grope for the starting point it hits me that I still hardly know Sarah. She hardly knows me. She definitely doesn't know Walter. This is not right. I'm going to have to figure this one out on my own. But I have to tell her something now. I can't show up here and just mumble and leave. "Um, I want to tell you something."

"Okay."

Might as well be something I need to tell her anyway. "I'm really, well . . . I think you're great." I look at the fireplace. Then I look back at her to see how that went.

"Ray, you are so sweet."

I know I am red now. I stand up. "I really like you, too."

Sarah gets out of the chair and walks over. "Now, I didn't say I *liked* you."

I didn't expect that at all. "What?"

She smiles and her eyes shine. "Sorry. Couldn't resist. I like you, too. You've got to have figured that out."

"Yeah. Sure. Wow, you can really shake a guy up with that teasing stuff."

She goes up on her toes, messing around. "It's something I do pretty well. That and motocross, of course."

I laugh, picturing Sarah in the X Games. "Wait till you see what I do pretty well."

Real coy she says, "Algebra?"

"No. Not algebra, smart-ass." I take both her hands. "How about I get you at eight tomorrow night? We'll go to a movie."

"Sounds divine."

"Okay. I better get going." I give her hands a squeeze and let go.

She jams her fists on her hips and puffs out her chest. "You come all the way over here, tell me you *really* like me, and there's no kiss? Didn't anyone ever teach you proper protocol for this sort of thing?"

This girl is too much. She is so cool. Everything I ever learned at those OLC parties comes rushing back. I kiss her and it goes a little bit longer than just a friendly peck, too. She walks me to the door and we're holding hands.

We stop on the porch. "Bye, Sarah. I'll see you tomorrow."

"Bye, Ray." She reels me in for a hug and whispers in my ear, "And good luck with whatever's going on. I'm thinking about you."

She is so smart. I fly home. I am like air.

After dinner, I do my homework. Things are definitely turning a corner. Sarah and I are finally really together. Malovic is put in his place. Looks like Robert and Rudy are going to get their butts in trouble. Ha, ha. And now maybe there's a chance Walter's coming around. He's the one who wanted to talk. The more I think about it, the more I can sense it's going to work out.

After about an hour of homework at the kitchen table I hear Walter's truck out front. It's easy to hear. He's beeping his horn like a maniac. My mother wrinkles her forehead at the noise. "It's nine o'clock," she says. "Be back by eleven, please."

"I'll be in way before then. We're just going to Howard's." I kiss Mom a quick one and grab a jacket. It's still cool, but it's not that biting chill any more. It's starting to warm up.

"All right, Ray-mon-do!" Walter messes up my hair when I slide into the front seat. He seems really up. Not like this afternoon at all.

"Hey." I figure I'll wait till we're at Howard's for the big talk.

He peers out his window and up at the sky. Then he looks at a watch on his wrist. I don't think I've ever seen him wear a watch before. "Time to go," he says. "I got a surprise for you." He pulls out, tires squealing, and heads toward Bridgeton.

"Hey, man. You're going the wrong way."

"Don't worry. We'll get to Howard's. This won't take that long." The truck engine roars as we zoom up the highway.

"What won't?"

"Kicking their black butts."

chapter twenty-eight
SHOWDOWN

Everything stops. I feel almost weightless, like faint. "What are you talking about?"

Walter stares intently out the windshield at the traffic ahead. "I set it up so you can kick Rudy's sorry butt."

"What?"

He glances over at me. "I called Rudy and told him you wanted to get him back for getting Seven on you." Walter must see the shock on my face. He nods and smiles. "Teddy saw that little incident with you and Seven and then we checked into it. That's what happened. Rudy set you up."

Real slow I say, "You called Rudy?"

We're driving fast. Walter is grinning. "Ray, he actually paid Seven fifty bucks. Can you believe that? I called that skinny pipe cleaner-looking punk and told him he couldn't pull this crap on you without getting it back. I told him to be there or else."

Walter is into this. His eyes are almost glowing. "Walter, don't be crazy. Stop the car."

"Too late, Ray. They asked for it."

I sit up. He's really going to do this. I've got to talk him down and out of it quick. "You're gonna get in all kinds of trouble. Rudy probably told everybody."

"No he didn't. I told Mr. Pipe Cleaner that if he said *one* word to anyone else besides his driver, I'd find him personal-like and beat the crap out of him."

"His driver?"

Walter pulls over to the curb and honks his horn hard three times. "Yeah. I figured he'd need somebody to drive him to the hospital so I told him to bring somebody along for that."

I haven't even noticed which way we've been going. We're in front of Lutch's Bar. I move for the door. "I'm out of here."

Walter leans towards me. "No. You stick." His voice is cold.

Four guys come weaving out of Lutch's together. I know them. Two go to OLC. Another guy is one of Walter's shop buddies. Teddy Turkowski is the fourth. Lutch's doesn't mind serving beer to anybody.

Teddy presses his face to my window so his nose is squished up. "Hey, Ray-Ray," he says, grinning.

I look back at Walter again. His eyes are fixed on me.

Walter's boys pile into the truck bed. After they get in, he pushes back into his seat and throws the transmission into drive. He smiles all smug. "Reinforcements," he says. "Just in case Rudy doesn't believe in keeping a secret. Hey, if you're lucky, Robert might drive him, and you can watch me beat his butt. I feel like beating somebody's butt tonight." He guns the truck and does a quick U-turn heading back toward Greenville.

I keep my voice steady, but it takes some effort. "Drop me off at my house."

Walter talks all matter-of-fact, "Sorry, Ray. We're doing this. If you don't get them back, they'll know they can get you again and again. Any of us. All of us."

I shake my head. "They? Seven hit me once and he's getting expelled."

This seems to infuriate him. "You gotta give it back. I'm not going to let them do this to you."

"Walter, who is 'them'? I told you—Seven's expelled already."

He looks back and forth at the road and at me. "And Rudy? And Robert? What about them?!"

"Malovic and Gallo already know about them."

We stop at a traffic light. Walter's face is bathed in red from the light. "Yeah, right. Gallo and Malovic. They're going to do a lot. Ray, you don't understand this situation and I do. You're book-smart. Not street-smart."

"You're street-smart? You live on a farm."

Walter yells, "I know what I'm doing!"

"Well you're gonna do it without me. This is whacked." I unlock my door and grab the handle and open it. Walter shoots across the seat, grabs my wrist, and yanks me back. His hands are big, with huge broad knuckles. I try to pull out of his grip, but I can't.

"No, Ray! If you don't show tonight, it'll just happen another night. They're not gonna forget about it and neither am I."

I sit back in the seat. Walter lets go of my arm. The light changes. "Close the door," he says.

I slide over to get out. Walter slams on the gas and we peel out from the light. The car swerves across two lanes. Teddy howls, "Yeehaw! All right!"

Walter yells, "Close the damn door!"

The door is flapping. I have to lean in, then reach over and shut it so I don't fall out or get smacked. I can feel where his hand was on my wrist. We jet through the darkness. "You are losing it, man."

But Walter isn't listening. He makes the turn into the empty high school parking lot. He cruises the truck slowly to the rear of the lot. I hear movement behind me. The guys are crawling under a tarp.

We get to the utility road behind the school. Walter shuts the headlights off. He creeps the car even slower over the gravel till he's next to the field house. There are no lights back here. You can still see because of the parking lot lights and the lights down on the basketball courts and tennis courts. It's all in shadows, though.

Walter stops the truck. He stares at me across the seat,

not moving an inch. No expression. He's like a big stone block. "Time to get out, Ray." It's a command.

We both get out. A couple of giggles filter up from under the tarp. I can smell beer and smoke. Walter hisses, "Shut up. Stay under there till I tell you."

Teddy whispers, "Aye, aye, captain," and they all giggle again.

"There they are. Look." Walter points to a couple of cars parked by the fence. Two dark figures come walking slowly out from behind a yellow Camaro. One I can tell right away is Rudy. And then the other one walks into the light. It's Seven!

They walk over till they're about ten feet away and they stop. Rudy is half a step behind Seven's shoulder. Walter is smiling. "I thought you wasn't gonna show. Especially nice to see you here, Mr. Seven-Eleven."

Seven smirks. "I'm *real* glad to see you, Walter boy. I've been waiting to see you."

"Hold on." Walter points at Rudy. "Rudy Kazootie. You and Ray-Ray do it up. Me and Seven will stand by and get into it after, if he's a good *boy*."

Seven has his left hand deep in his pocket. Guys say he carries a knife. He says all smooth, "Now that's not the way we figured it exactly. C'mon," he calls out. Rudy's got this huge smile on his face. From behind the equipment shed, three other guys come walking out. It's Rudy's boys from the stands. A couple of guys about my size and one smaller, chunky guy.

Walter makes this little *tsk, tsk* noise. "Oh, you boys are so naughty. Didn't nobody teach you to play fair? Hey fellas! Our playmates are here!" Four big Polack boys tumble out of the back of the truck. I see three baseball bats.

My heart is racing. We're all gonna get killed here. I gotta do something. I take a couple of shaky steps forward. "Hold it. This is really messed up. We're gonna get nothing but trouble from this."

Rudy is on his toes, bouncing from foot to foot. "Oh, you little pussy. You right. You gonna get trouble. Big trouble. And we gonna give it to you!"

Walter yells at me, "Knock it off, Ray!"

Talk slow. Stay cool. My heart is trying to get out of my chest, though. Nobody moves because everybody realizes things are pretty even up, except for the bats, but then the Polacks don't know what the brothers got with them. I've got to keep talking. If we're talking nobody's swinging. I concentrate on Walter.

"Walter. Come on. Let's go."

Walter hisses, "I'm trying to help you here, Ray. Don't let these dopes get between us."

Rudy, stupid as ever, laughs. "Don't get *between* yous? You into each other?"

Walter rounds on him. "Shut up, nigger!"

You can feel the air being sucked in by all eleven sets of lungs. The word floats there. Then Seven tilts his head slowly. He speaks real soft. "You goin' be so, so sorry you said that." He walks forward.

"Cool out, Walter," I say coming closer to him. If Seven goes after him, I'm gonna have to help. Somehow. The Polack boys are looking at Walter for a signal. Teddy lifts the bat up to his shoulder. Walter brings his left foot forward. It's gonna start.

Then we all hear it at the same time.

A car engine.

Everybody looks back to the parking lot. Two headlights move slowly across the lot and then swing toward us. It's like the car is patrolling and just spotted us. Like the cops. I'm ready to run. The car reaches the gravel road. And the lights go out.

Cops wouldn't be turning the lights out.

The car grinds to a stop right at the edge of the dirt. An old, light brown station wagon. Rusted. Dented up. The front license plate is hanging all crooked from a piece of wire. Doors on both sides swing open and four guys climb out.

chapter twenty-nine
BLACK AND WHITE

I can see the huge bodies clear as anything in the weird light. The three Hayes brothers. Al, Jamal, and Tyrone, and this guy from the football team, Darnell Garnet. Now another guy comes out of the way back. Darnell's little brother, six-feet-one-hundred-and-ninety-pound James. I've played ball in ROCK with both the Garnets. Then one last guy. Winnie.

Rudy is cheering, "All right, brothers! Let's get it on. My man, Winnie, Jamal, Al, Dar-nell!"

The guys behind Rudy are slapping hands. The chunky guy chants in a nursery rhyme cadence, "Honkies gon-na di-ie. Honkies gon-na di-ie." Seven rubs his chin and grins. He eyes me and nods his head a couple of times. My whole body goes cold.

The guys from the car are walking across the field real slow. Walter looks back at me with his mouth half open. This was not in his plan. Then he recovers. His eyes narrow. He tightens his fists. "Get ready, Ray. We can still take them."

The little group keeps walking till they're in the middle

of us. There are now eleven black guys. Winnie steps to the front. His face is a blank. He says to me, "Hey, man."

I try to speak, but all I can manage is a nod.

A little half smile crosses his face. "We gonna play some ball. You wanna play?"

What does that mean? Rudy's boys and the Polacks look at each other. They don't get it either.

Tyrone steps toward me. My old coach from ROCK. He's like a giant. Bigger than ever. "Ray-Ray, what's going on?" He puts his hand out for a bump.

I bring my hand up all shaky and bump him lightly. He has a basketball under one arm. "Hey, Tyrone," I say. The words barely make it out.

Seven pimp rolls toward Tyrone. He's so close I can smell his aftershave. "Hey. What's this?"

Tyrone looks down at Seven. "Get out of my face before I knock you back to Sunday."

Seven tilts his head and sneers. "Who you talkin' to?"

Darnell moves in. "He's talking to you, little boy. Back off."

Seven dips his left hand into his jacket pocket. Darnell sees it. "Oh, you got your little can opener wit' you? You try and cut me. Give me an excuse."

Seven doesn't move. He glances around to see if anyone's backing him up. They aren't. All his boys are sliding off to the sides. Darnell sees Seven hesitate. He says, "You *better* not mess with me."

Seven takes a step back. His hand is out of his pocket now. Darnell stays right near him and Seven looks like a skinny Munchkin in *The Wizard of Oz*. He takes two more steps back. Rudy is even farther away than he is. The Polack boys have done some moving too. Toward the truck.

Darnell looks over at Tyrone like Seven isn't even there. "Tyrone, we gonna play or what?"

Tyrone says, "Yeah. C'mon."

The six of them start walking over to the courts. No one is moving except them. No one knows what to do. They pass right on through.

Then Al looks back at me. Real casual he says, "C'mon, Ray, let's get it rollin'."

Tyrone says, "Yeah, Ray. Let's do it."

I glance at Walter. He's is so white under the light. It looks like all the color's been washed out. I turn and follow Tyrone.

Walter bellows, "What!" I turn back around. His face is creased up like he's in pain. "That's it? You let them kick your butt and then you're gonna play ball with them?"

I shake my head. "You don't get it."

Walter hisses, "Get what? This is simple, Ray. You gotta make a choice. Is it gonna be black or is it gonna be white?"

That's how he sees it. That's how he's always gonna see it. I turn and start down toward the court again.

Walter yells after me, "That's right! Walk away from your own people."

I spin back and shout, "No! Don't twist it! You're here to hurt somebody. I'm going down there, because that's where they're playing ball. *That's* the real choice! Now, what are you going to do?"

He looks over at the black guys frozen in place. He looks at the Polack boys. Then back to me. A little look flashes across his face. Like a sad, almost pleading look and just as quick he turns his back on me and walks toward the truck. He spits out the words. "C'mon. It smells bad around here."

The Polack boys jump back in the truck. The engine roars and Walter peels out. Gravel sprays from the back tires. Exhaust and dirt hang in the air as the car speeds off into the dark.

Walter's gone. My old buddy, Walter. Big ol' funny, freckle-faced Walter.

I start walking down to the court again. Rudy waits until the truck is a good hundred yards away and then starts yelling after it, "Yeah. You better run out of here, you yellow punks."

I quicken my pace. I don't hear anybody right behind me, so I sneak a look back. Seven is in the Camaro with the chunky guy driving. They cruise up to Rudy. Seven reaches out and grabs a handful of Rudy's hair and jerks him down toward the window.

"Give me my money now, you little pissant," he snarls.

"But, Seven, man. You didn't, I mean, nothing happened."

"Mess with me!" Seven yells and slaps Rudy's face hard with his free hand. "Give me it!"

Rudy fumbles around in his pockets and gives Seven something. "Screw you," Seven says. He pushes Rudy, and the car roars away. The second car follows right behind. All that's left up there is the sorry-looking station wagon. And Rudy. He straightens his shirt out and smooths his jacket. It's clear he doesn't know what to do. Finally he comes walking over to the courts.

Everybody's shooting it up already when I go through the fence gate and under the court lights. Now that I'm safe, my body is shaking. Al comes over and claps me on the shoulder. "What's up, Ray?"

I try to hold myself still, but I have to laugh at how cool Al is acting. Like nothing happened. "Going to play some ball, I guess."

He laughs. "I guess so."

A few seconds later Rudy comes striding down the hill. Tyrone meets him at the gate, blocking the entry with his big frame. "Go home, Rudy."

"What?"

"I said, 'Go home.'"

Rudy just stares for a second. Looking at everyone on the court. Then he backs up. "You guys are nuts. What you doin' with this white boy?"

Tyrone snorts. "You know, Rudy. You a punk. We got nuthin' to say to you."

Rudy flails his arms around. "What! You gonna kiss the white master's behind, too?"

Tyrone moves up the hill toward him. "No, I'm gonna kick the dopey black boy's behind!" Jamal steps over and puts a hand on him.

"Forget him, man." Then he says to Rudy. "Go home, Rudy. You ain't runnin' with us."

I just stand there watching it and loving it. Rudy sees they're for real. He pivots around and pimp rolls off up the hill. He walks through the grass to the parking lot. "Suckers!" he yells over his shoulder.

James is watching Rudy pimp rolling. "Looks like an ostrich that got his butt nipped."

There's laughs all around on that one. "That's original," Darnell says.

I laugh. And keep laughing. Oh, god. What a relief to laugh. I say, "Tyrone, man. Guys. Thanks. You were like the calvary or something showing up like that."

Tyrone doesn't smile. "No biggie, Ray. Buncha chumps. All of them."

My breathing is coming back to normal. My heart is slowing down. "How'd you know about this?"

Winnie nods at Tyrone. "Tell him, man."

Tyrone shrugs. "He ain't goin' believe it."

"What?" I look around from guy to guy. It's quiet.

Then Al says, "Who ain't here?"

I glance around again. "I don't know."

"No, think about it. Who wasn't wit' Rudy? Who's *always* wit' Rudy?"

Then it hits me. "Get out."

Tyrone sees my face and smiles. "Serious."

I don't even have to say it out loud, but I do anyway. "Robert?"

"Yep."

I shake my head. "No."

Tyrone glances up at the sky. I look too. Stars. It's nice to see stars. I never even noticed them being out tonight till now. Maybe they weren't before.

Tyrone goes on. "Yeah. Believe that? He calls me this afternoon. Calls *me* on the phone. Like Robert and I are pals always calling each other! He don't say hello or nothing. You know the way he is. Just that little froggy voice on the phone, 'You should check out the action behind the field house tonight at nine thirty.' I say, 'What are you talking about? Don't be stupid! What action?'"

Tyrone makes his voice sound like a frog, "'They goin' jump Ray-Ray.' That's all he said and hung up."

Robert. Unbelievable.

Tyrone says, "I figured he wouldn't be making it up."

So, Robert finally had to move off of Rudy to do the right thing. And I had to move off of Walter to do the same. A brotherhood of actions. Of deeds.

"Yeah, it's always a good time to play some ball anyway," Winnie says all sly.

I turn to Winnie. "And what are you doing here? I thought you were still PO'd at me about Stacey."

"Nah, I thought about it and figured you was just bein' stupid. Besides I heard you didn't get nothin', so—"

The other guys start howling, but a loud shout echoes down from the parking lot. "Hey, what are you kids doin' down there? It's late! Get home! Don't you have homes?"

Tyrone says, "I know that dopey voice."

Pruze comes walking down the hill. He's got cut-off shorts on and a ski vest. Typical hot dresser Pruze. He calls over, "Hey, Snow White and the, what—one, two, three—six crows. We need to lighten this action up."

"Oh, man. The Polish Pickle is here." Tyrone makes his lemon-sucking face.

"You know about this too?" I ask.

"Yeah, old son. My man Tyrone told me to meet over here, but I figured I'd hang back. I didn't want to spoil the color scheme. Also figured I'd be there to call 9-1-1 if I needed to."

Tyrone says, "Yeah, you was just scared someone would actually do something and you might get your good looks all messed up."

"Well, there was that too." Pruze smiles and pushes his hair back.

"Hey. Let's play already. We're here now," says Darnell. He puts a shot up and in. "You boys gotta practice, got the states coming up."

Tyrone passes me the ball. "Fire it up, Ray."

I look at these guys and I can't stop smiling. But I feel this deep bad thing at the same time. I had to walk away from Walter. I guess for good.

And what'll I say to Robert when I see him? Maybe he wouldn't mind some help with his assignments. I don't know if he'd go for it, but I figure I got to at least ask now or something. Who knows anymore with Robert?

A shout breaks through my thinking. It's Al. He's sounding impatient. "C'mon, Ray. Buss it, man. You make it, you take it."

I spin the ball around in my hand. It's smooth and worn. It's been in a lot of games. I go up straight and let it go soft, with the backspin against my fingers. I watch it arcing toward the rim under the lights. It feels good. It feels right.

Piff!